"You didn't b... We're leavin...

"Your choice, Commander." Bolan turned away and headed toward the Huey.

Unable to stop herself, Alireza raced after the warrior, laid a hand on his shoulder, then threw the weight of her whole body into a palm-heel strike.

The Executioner's head was rocked back by the blow, and he sank into a defensive crouch. Tension ran through the group of men ringing them. Some of the mercenaries had already brandished handguns. Grimaldi had his pistol cocked and ready.

A trickle of blood leaked down Bolan's chin, and he wiped it away with the back of his hand. Sudden violence between the two groups was balanced on a razor's edge.

One false move and the mission would be scrubbed before it could get off the ground.

MACK BOLAN®

The Executioner

#125 Dead Man's Tale	Stony Man Doctrine
#126 Death Wind	Terminal Velocity
#127 Kill Zone	Resurrection Day
#128 Sudan Slaughter	Dirty War
#129 Haitian Hit	Flight 741
#130 Dead Line	Dead Easy
#131 Ice Wolf	Sudden Death
#132 The Big Kill	Rogue Force
#133 Blood Run	Tropic Heat
#134 White Line War	Fire in the Sky
#135 Devil Force	Anvil of Hell
#136 Down and Dirty	Flash Point
#137 Battle Lines	Flesh and Blood
#138 Kill Trap	Moving Target
#139 Cutting Edge	Tightrope
#140 Wild Card	Blowout
#141 Direct Hit	Blood Fever
#142 Fatal Error	Knockdown
#143 Helldust Cruise	Assault
#144 Whipsaw	Backlash
#145 Chicago Payoff	Siege
#146 Deadly Tactics	Blockade
#147 Payback Game	Evil Kingdom
#148 Deep and Swift	Counterblow
#149 Blood Rules	Hardline
#150 Death Load	Firepower
#151 Message to Medellín	
#152 Combat Stretch	
#153 Firebase Florida	
#154 Night Hit	
#155 Hawaiian Heat	
#156 Phantom Force	
#157 Cayman Strike	
#158 Firing Line	
#159 Steel and Flame	
#160 Storm Warning	
#161 Eye of the Storm	

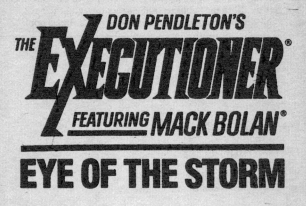

DON PENDLETON'S
THE EXECUTIONER®
FEATURING MACK BOLAN®

EYE OF THE STORM

A GOLD EAGLE BOOK FROM
WORLDWIDE®

TORONTO • NEW YORK • LONDON
AMSTERDAM • PARIS • SYDNEY • HAMBURG
STOCKHOLM • ATHENS • TOKYO • MILAN
MADRID • WARSAW • BUDAPEST • AUCKLAND

First edition May 1992

ISBN 0-373-61161-7

Special thanks and acknowledgment to
Mel Odom for his contribution to this work.

EYE OF THE STORM

Printed in U.S.A.

When you see a rattlesnake poised to strike you, you do not wait until he has struck before you crush him.
—Franklin D. Roosevelt
September 11, 1941

They say history repeats itself, and I'm in no position to dispute that statement. Yet why can't humankind learn from its mistakes? This viper *must* be crushed ruthlessly. We must not let it rise up—again.
—Mack Bolan

To the men and women of
the Desert Storm allied forces

PROLOGUE

Riyadh, Saudi Arabia

CNN correspondent Dwight Meacham ran as if he were still a collegiate track-and-field contender instead of a thirty-five-year-old man. Scud missiles—he couldn't tell how many—continued to strike the Saudi airfield. His right hand still fisted the microphone while his left secured the battery pack at the back of his waist. Lungs already seared by the burning need for oxygen, he threw himself the final few yards and skidded into the scant cover provided by a cinder-block bunker.

A fresh eruption of dirt, dust and tarmac chunks showered over him. He held his hand over his head and coughed. Tears streamed from his eyes. Mud smeared his palm as he rubbed it over his face. Meacham was startled to find blood mixed in there, as well. Fumbling for the jury-rigged military radio he'd bought on the black market that had sprung up in Saudi Arabia since the Gulf War, he peered around the corner of the bunker.

The onslaught of Scuds appeared to be slowing. The ground didn't tremble nearly as often. Patriot missiles spewed gray vapor trails across the blue sky, vanishing against the blinding eye of the noonday sun. The two missiles collided, the boom of their impact rolling like thunder.

Meacham tried not to think about the dead and dying that had to be spilled across the broken tarmac. Hands shaking from the near miss, he fitted the radio plug into his ear and cranked up the volume. News reports were broken up by static and the whining banshee wails of emergency rescue vehicles.

Sand sprayed over Meacham when Curtis Richards sprawled against the bunker beside him. The cameraman carried his camcorder tightly against his stomach.

"Is that camera okay?" Meacham asked.

"Oh, yeah," Richards replied. "Even as scared as I was that I was about to get my ass blown away out there, I didn't even want to face the alternative of bumming a camcorder from the U.S. Army."

"Get it ready. We're going on the air in a couple of minutes." Meacham cupped his hands and shouted through them. "Keeler, haul your ass out from under that jeep and get over here!"

The CNN sound man waved, then lugged his minisatellite case over to the bunker, pausing twice for ambulances.

"You ready, Keeler?"

The communications guy waved an all-clear as he continued to speak rapidly into the microphone hung in front of his face from the headset. He held up five fingers, ticked one of them off and sat beside the minisatellite dish, which projected toward a receiver thousands of miles out in space.

"Richards," Meacham said, "pan on my signal. First the airfield, then the sky. One finger, then two."

Richards nodded. The camcorder flared high-intensity light that drenched Meacham.

Keeler was down to three fingers, two, then one. Meacham struck a pose with the microphone in front of him. The earplug connecting the correspondent to CNN buzzed to harsh life. The anchor had cleared him for five minutes. He intended to buy more than that.

"We're here at an allied-occupied air base near Riyadh," Meacham said. "A Scud missile attack against allied forces took place—" he paused to look at his watch with authority "—at 12:07 p.m. Less than five minutes ago there was no death, no destruction here. Now emergency crews are strained, trying to take care of the wounded and the dead.

"Military commanders at the post are hesitant to estimate how high the death toll might run." He signaled Richards to pan out over the airfield. "Even in the blistering aftermath of the assault on allied bases in Kuwait, it appears the attack today took this base by surprise. The Patriot missile system seemed sluggish to respond. Once they did, though, American technology once more proved superior to anything the Iraqis have. However, the Scuds appeared in greater numbers than were anticipated.

"Following as it is on the heels of the brazen attacks against allied forces in Kuwait less than forty-eight hours ago, there can be no doubt that Khalid Shawiyya intends to take up the fight where his predecessor and mentor, Saddam Hussein, left off. The Middle East has a long history of retribution. Today, however, there appears to be a new cornerstone being laid.

"And it is being put down in our country, as well. At the same time as the attacks took place in Kuwait, there was a terrorist attack on the Persian Gulf War Memorial services on Sunday. Americans have been killed on American soil. Apparently Shawiyya is drawing no boundaries as far as his attempt at revenge for the Iraqi peoples is concerned. Senator Tim Kilkenny and others have been cold-bloodedly murdered by other terrorist groups.

"According to the Iraqi media, President Shawiyya is already taking credit for the terrorist strikes here and abroad. And he's promising more to come.

"From our sources in the Middle East who are watching for the insertion of American and allied troops, reports are dismal. Troop movement on the allied behalf is sluggish and slow. It might soon prove to be a case of too little too late.

"The assassination of Hamoud Jaluwi in Damascus by a supposed CIA agent could prove to be a pivotal turning point in this conflict. Although the assassin's identity is disputed by a number of parties, including Israel's own counterintelligence agency, the Mossad, the Syrians are making decisions for themselves. In last year's war the country was barely held in check by the strong guiding hand of its president, Hafez Assad. Now, it seems, even Assad will be unable to head off the overspill of violence spreading throughout his nation."

Another Patriot intercepted a descending Scud hundreds of feet overhead, and the resulting explosion was deafening. Meacham went facedown into the sand, followed a heartbeat later by Richards and Keeler. The reporter grabbed his microphone and pushed himself into a kneeling position. Metal bits pinged off the cinder-block walls of the bunker and thudded into the sand. One piece, fast and burning hot, ricocheted off his bare ankle. He glanced at Keeler.

The communications man crawled back toward his gear, checked the dials, then flipped a handful of toggles. "Sorry. I guess we lost them."

"Get them back as soon as you can." Meacham brushed sand from his face. The toll from the sleepless hours he'd spent wandering around the allied airfield rattled inside him like a stick against the bare ribs of a skeleton. He pushed out an angry breath and calmed himself.

Looking at the black haze from fires and explosions staining the blue sky, he noted the flickering flashes from the jet fighters streaking high overhead. He decided not to let the loss of the signal and his chance to seize more airtime bother him.

From everything he'd seen, the world was going to war, might even hover on the edge of complete destruction if it didn't go ahead and make the jump. There would be plenty of chances for stories.

He remembered that war was one of the four horsemen of the apocalypse, and for a moment he thought he could hear thundering hoofbeats in the distance. He shivered and turned his attention to his crew.

Somewhere behind war, famine and pestilence, Meacham knew death was a pale rider dressed in black. And he didn't doubt the presence of the elemental force sweeping in over the land. Desert Storm had only marked the beginning of the conflagration.

1

The British-made Challenger Main Battle Tank squatted on the wreckage of the Volkswagen minivan like a mechanical predator over the torn body of a fresh kill. Broken bricks and glass from the small shop it had charged through less than a minute ago covered the hull and decks. Servos whined as the turret continued to come around. Flames still writhed around the corpse of another vehicle that lay in a twisted heap on the war-torn Kuwait City street.

Mack Bolan raised his M-16 and raked a withering burst of gunfire across the Chobham armor protecting the gunner and wheelman. If a British crew had been inside, there would have been no hesitation before the 120 mm gun fired again. Instead, the crew manning the tank now didn't have the confidence in the armor plating to react without flinching.

Talia Alireza was at the Executioner's side, lean and feminine despite the dark camouflage fatigues she wore. Her gloved hands were curled around a chopped-down Remington Model 870 12-gauge shotgun. Her tawny blond hair was pulled back into a ponytail by a leather thong. Her eyes, as cool and calculating as gun sights, took in the combat situation. Like Bolan, she wore a crimson scarf tied around her upper left arm to identify herself as a friendly.

"Striker!" Jack Grimaldi yelled from the receiver of Bolan's ear-throat headset.

Still on the move, Bolan paused to feed a new magazine into his assault rifle and load a white phosphorous grenade into the M-203 slung under the M-16. "Go," he said when he hit the transmit button.

Distinctive reports from Grimaldi's Barrett M-82 .50-caliber sniper rifle punctuated the confusion of noise caused by the tank and Scud missiles descending on the city like carrion fowl. "You got a dozen or so ground troops moving into your sector," the Stony Man flyboy said. "And that's only the tally I got from the last count."

Alireza's smooth voice flowed into the silence before the Executioner could respond. "Jimoh?" The name was a question.

"Seventeen, and counting." The voice was deep, loose and ready.

Grimaldi's weapon banged out another round.

"Keep me apprised of any newcomers," Bolan responded as he took cover behind the rear wall of a bombed-out building. "Get as many faces as you can. We've got some Kremlin jokers in the deck."

"Affirmative. Eagle One out."

The British tank rolled off the corpse of the minivan, the treads locking as it settled into firing position.

Bolan's mind was filled with questions concerning the presence of the Russians he and Talia had run into only moments ago. So far the developing Middle East campaign had shown only the signs of the new Iraqi leader's aggressions. There had been no doubts in the minds of the Stony Man intelligence people that other Arab countries were involved, as well. But no one had suspected Russian participation.

The 120 mm cannon roared.

The Executioner had the momentary impression of a belch of flame coming from the wide-bore muzzle, then he was going to ground behind the wall. The round slammed through the first wall, then went slightly off-center as it continued on through the one Bolan used for shelter.

His hearing blanked out immediately. Concrete dust, splinters and chunks of other debris rained down on him. His breath left his lungs from the pounding he received. Bruised ribs promised more pain to come. His numbed hand found his assault rifle almost by instinct. He coughed as he looked up through the smoky haze left by the explosive force that had whipped through the walls. Down the street the tank was on the move again, already targeting him, the turret whining while it was reaimed.

"Striker?" Grimaldi called.

"I'm mobile," Bolan said. He reached up, used his body as a lever and shifted the concrete blocks off his back, shoulders and legs. His head pounded, and his ribs tried to tighten up as he sucked his breath back in. His hands looked scraped, raw and bloody as he fisted the M-16/M-203 over-and-under combination. So far the pain hadn't settled in, but he knew it was coming. He sighted, then triggered the grenade launcher.

The phosphorous round streaked through the air and impacted against the Challenger. An explosion of white-hot flame engulfed the front of the tank. It would prove negligible against the armor, but the novice crew inside couldn't know that.

More Scuds continued to bombard the city. Vibrations rumbled along the streets, jarring loose fragments of glass from broken windows in the abandoned buildings.

A figure came into view in front of Bolan as the Executioner got to his feet. The warrior quickly checked for the identifying crimson armband. There was none. He lifted the M-16 and dispatched the black-clad man with a pair of 3-round bursts.

Alireza had taken cover across the street. He saw her now, hunkered down behind the building she'd chosen for protection. The Remington shotgun was slung upside down over her shoulder. A Hämmerli Model 208 target pistol was gripped confidently in both hands, and she squeezed off shot after shot with slow deliberation.

Bolan noted the open slot in front of the driver's position. One of the .22LR rounds struck sparks from the edge of the slot. Two more flat cracks from the pistol followed. Neither of them hit metal, and the Executioner didn't believe for a moment that the woman had missed the entire tank. Then, abruptly, the Challenger heeled around, one set of treads driving deeply into the roadway.

Alireza had chosen her armament with care. A heavier caliber slug wouldn't have proved as dangerous to the tank crew inside. But the .22LRs had a tendency to bounce. The effectiveness of her abilities showed when the tank plowed into another building and crashed halfway through, bringing down the second story on top of it.

A shadow drifted into Alireza's background. Bolan raised the M-16 to his shoulder and dropped the sights over the attacker's face. But Jimoh had already warned the woman over the ear-throat headset frequency.

Responding immediately, she spun around and dropped to one knee. Her left hand raked a throwing knife from a calf-high boot top. The blade glittered through the air and easily pierced the man's throat. Before her attacker had time to take more than two stumbling steps backward, Alireza had a SIG-Sauer P-226 in her fist. A trio of shots punched the man to the ground.

Bolan released the trigger and raised the barrel of the M-16. The woman was full of surprises.

The bombardment of the city seemed to slow. Patriot missiles arced white trails overhead and tracked down targets, which burst in the air like overripe fruit.

Across the street Alireza reloaded the Hämmerli and put it away. ''Kuwait City isn't the only target for Shawiyya's

Scuds," she said over the headset. "Strikes have also been launched against Israel and Saudi Arabia."

Her information told Bolan she was hard-wired into at least two radio frequencies. It proved that despite her willingness to participate in the strikes against the Iraqi dictator, she hadn't entirely trusted the situation.

With a crunching wrench the big British tank freed itself from the wreckage of the building. It trundled backward while the turret spun around. The access hatch opened. An Arab in desert camous pulled himself along the exposed portion of the tank's deck and tried to settle in behind the 7.62 mm machine gun mounted coaxially with the 120 mm cannon. Another man bolted for the machine gun mounted on the commander's cupola.

The Executioner saw the smear of blood staining the forward gunner's face as he targeted the man through the open sights of the M-16.

The machine gun opened up at once, and 7.62 mm bullets spewed randomly. Rounds thudded into the street and chopped up the sides of buildings. The gunner kept the trigger locked and hunkered down as low as he could. Brass casings spun and sparkled in the hot sun. A moment later the second gunner joined the first.

Bolan fired one single-shot, placing his rounds with deliberation. The metal shield covering the lead gunner left little to aim at. Twice his bullets tore through exposed cloth but didn't score in the flesh beneath. Bright pain zigzagged through his ankle as he shifted his weight. It didn't feel broken, so he ignored it.

The tank barreled toward him, vibrations shivering through the street under the Executioner's feet.

"It's you they're after, Striker," Alireza transmitted.

Bolan didn't respond. He knew it was true. Somehow the covert operation Stony Man Farm had fielded into the explosive mix in the Middle East had been compromised. The

Russians came to mind again. The Arab countries might not have had the capabilities to tear through American military intelligence, but the Soviets did. The mission had definitely taken on a different spin.

In the distance the Scuds shelling Kuwait City sounded like muted drumbeats. The air crackled overhead with American and allied aircraft moving the attack onto a higher plane.

Bolan turned and ran. If the assault team was truly single-minded of purpose, he could provide his people a chance to take the behemoth down.

The Challenger's main gun belched thunder behind him. The 120 mm round impacted against the street and ripped out a hole large enough to bury a small car in.

Unable to keep upright, the Executioner went down, used one hand to turn the fall into a more or less controlled roll and got back onto his feet. He drove his legs hard against the cracked, paved surface, negotiating piles of rubble with hurdling jumps.

Despite the tonnage the British tank gained on him. With a top speed of thirty-five miles an hour, it could easily outdistance the Executioner on the straightaway. And it didn't have to deal with the rubble strewing the street. It simply rolled over it.

Perspiration fogged Bolan's vision for a moment when the salt burned his eyes. He hit the transmit button on his headset and called Alireza's code name. "Valkyrie."

"Go," she replied.

Autofire chewed through the noise of tank treads, letting the Executioner know that the ambush had added new fronts. He threw himself suddenly to the left, ducking into the crumbled remains of an alley that looked too small to admit the tank. His shoulder thudded into a cracked wall only inches from a shattered window gleaming with jagged shards of glass.

Bolan keyed the transmit button again. "The place where I took down the first two men. Where we met."

"Yes."

"There was a package you might find useful," he said, not mentioning the LAW rockets they'd discovered there in case the assault team was monitoring their frequency.

"I know the one you're talking about. I'm almost there now. Valkyrie out."

A scream of tortured metal sounded behind Bolan. Machine gun fire rattled along the alley walls. He paused, brought the M-16 to his shoulder and focused on the forward gunner as the Challenger surged into the alley like a metal tidal wave.

Bricks and cinder blocks shattered as the tank powered into the narrow passage. The blunted treads scraped more debris from the broken walls, stone crushing to powder as the war machine rolled over.

For a moment the gunner behind the lead weapon was bounced out into the open. Bolan didn't hesitate. The distance was something less than thirty feet. His finger curled around the M-16's trigger, and he squeezed off a round. The first bullet took the man in the forehead; the second found his open mouth.

The soldier's body tumbled from the Challenger like a sack of grain and disappeared under the driving treads. But the tank didn't pause. Instead, it lumbered on with gnashing of gears and gained speed as the walls came tumbling down around it.

Bolan faced the other end of the alley and sprinted for all he was worth. Less than forty feet away the passage dead-ended with a swaying wooden fence more than eight feet high. Piles of refuse and debris lay heaped in front of it.

"Eagle One, this is Striker."

"Go, Striker." Jack Grimaldi's voice sounded tense. Hollow booms of the big Barrett .50-caliber rifle echoed around him.

"Contact Desert Lighting Base and get those people up here. Tell Desert Lightning Two he's in charge till I'm able to take over. He's to use his discretion." Desert Lightning Base was a contingent of almost eighteen hundred Special Forces fighters who had been secretly inserted near Kuwait City. They were a presidential surprise package awaiting an opportune moment to shut down Iraqi President Khalid Shawiyya's dreams of a Middle East conquest. Desert Lightning Two was the strong-willed Lieutenant Colonel Joshua Eldridge who, until only a few short hours ago, had been their commanding officer.

"Affirmative. Eagle One out."

Bolan plowed through the piles of refuse, slammed his body into the unsteady fence and pulled himself up. Garbage spilled down below him. The fence wavered uncertainly. For a moment he was sure the structure would topple over with him and leave him unprotected against the Challenger. Miraculously it held. He threw himself over the other side and landed on his feet. His injured ankle tried to go out from under him, but he forced it to hold up.

Maps of the surrounding city cycled through the Executioner's mind. He'd redrawn them and added footnotes to what already existed as he acquired new knowledge.

The alley dead-ended against a street that had once been a main artery of the city before war had reshaped lives and topography. Rusting automobiles showed signs of last year's bombings, as well as fresh scars from the past few minutes. Some of the shop windows flanking the broken sidewalks had been boarded over. Most of them, though, still gaped obscenely. Only picked-over goods remained.

At the east end of the street a U.S. Army two-and-a-half-ton truck made the turn onto the thoroughfare. Gears ground as the driver picked up speed.

Waiting in the shadows of the alley, Bolan let the big truck pass by, shouldered the M-16, then pursued. He felt the earthquake of movement behind him, signaling the tank's full-tilt lunge at the wooden fence. The barrier exploded, unable to contain the force. Broken wooden slats skittered across the street.

The Executioner ran all out, closing the distance separating him from the deuce-and-a-half with muscle-straining effort. He watched the GI behind the steering wheel notice him in the side mirror's reflection with an incredulous look. Then the soldier's attention shifted onto the tank becoming visible behind the truck.

Bolan grabbed the mirror and hauled himself up onto the running board beside the truck's cab. He unleathered the Eagle and screwed the barrel into the young soldier's neck, but made his voice easy when he spoke. "I'm Colonel Rance Pollock, United States Army, Corporal, but you're going to have to take my word for that at the moment."

The corporal nodded. "Yes, sir. Be glad to."

Bolan left the muzzle of the .44 Magnum where it was. There was no need to take any more chances than necessary, and the big gun guaranteed he'd keep the soldier's attention. "Take the right turn."

The deuce-and-a-half heeled over at once. Bearings grumbled and the transmission popped in protest.

The tank took a wide loop as the driver struggled to bring it under control. With only one set of treads digging into the pavement, it came around. Machine gun fire from the rear gunner slammed into the back of the truck. Tarp shredded under the hail of 7.62 mm rounds, leaping and jumping as following rounds caught the loose folds again. A corner of the Challenger smacked into an abandoned building.

Brickwork crumbled, shuddered and rained down over the rear gunner in a stone deluge that washed the man away before he saw it coming.

Bolan worked the door release and let himself inside. "Stop the truck."

The corporal did with a suddenness that almost caught Bolan off guard. He banged into the open door and almost lost his grip as it rebounded into him again. "Out. Now."

"Yes, sir." The corporal slid across the seat and let himself out the other side.

Bolan hit the clutch, thumbed the starter button and listened to the big power pack roar to life. "What are you hauling, Corporal?" He slapped the stick shift into first gear.

"Building supplies," the soldier answered. "Materials to patch up the airport the terrorists took out a couple of days ago."

Bolan nodded and stepped on the accelerator. He brought the big truck around and bounced over the debris in the side street. Rolling at speed now, he clutched and shifted up into second gear. The steering column jarred as the wheels pulled over the uneven surface. He cut back onto the primary street with a shrill of rubber.

The tank had broken free of the building rubble and was gaining momentum again. The Executioner wasn't sure how many tanks the terrorist forces had acquired during their latest attempt to break through Kuwait City defenses, but he knew how much damage even one of them could do to allied perimeters. The makeshift hospital for allied wounded was only a few blocks away.

He shifted into third gear and pulled the truck toward a collision path with the tank. The Challenger's main gun belched flame. Immediately the upper back half of the truck jumped in response. Bolan felt the impact all along the drive train. He clamped his hands on the steering wheel. The tank swelled into view on the other side of the truck's windshield.

"Striker?" Alireza called.

"Go," he answered.

"What is your position?"

"South, along the alley."

"I'll be there in seconds."

Even with the load of building supplies, Bolan knew the deuce-and-a-half's tonnage was nowhere near the British tank's. But he hoped to slow down the crew, buy his group some time.

He floored the accelerator. The distance separating the two metal giants became measured in feet and not yards. He knew he'd never get the truck up to fourth gear.

The tank slowed to a stop, which Bolan assumed was to allow the gun crew to reload. A trained crew could reload in something under ten seconds. Aiming was going to be point-blank. He slipped a knife free of his boot, jammed it through the accelerator and nailed it to the floor. He opened the door while he kept his other hand guiding the truck. Once he was sure the deuce-and-a-half wouldn't miss its target, he jumped.

The pavement came up with dizzying speed. As his palms slapped hard against the abrasive surface, he crumpled into a ball, intending to let his forward momentum carry him away from the crash zone. The M-16 caught on something, and he let the strap slide off his shoulder, already thinking of the Desert Eagle as his primary weapon.

His cheek stinging from contact with the street, Bolan came up on his knees facing the profile of the truck and tank as they collided. His right hand unleathered the .44 and settled it into the palm of his left hand while he searched for target acquisition.

The tank gunner fired the 120 mm gun at point-blank range. The round caught the truck in the midsection as the driving wheels and momentum propelled it up onto the low-slung Challenger. At ground zero the cannon shell detonated with as much implosion as explosion. Incendiaries flared in all directions. An exposed gas line under the truck caught fire, spread to the fuel tanks themselves and created another basso boom of destruction.

Bolan was buffeted by the concussive force warping back from the two vehicles. Sparks stung his skin; metal shrapnel scarred the street around him.

Gutted by the cannon round and the gasoline explosion, the deuce-and-a-half shivered like a dying metal dinosaur and fell over onto its side. Fire clung to the Challenger. One of the treads found purchase and forced the tank backward at an angle. The other tread flopped uselessly, severed by the explosion. Broken halfway down its length, the cannon hung at an odd angle while the turret servos stubbornly brought it around.

A lean feminine form vaulted over the broken fence and took up position at the side of the street.

Bolan regained his feet in a Weaver stance with the Desert Eagle trained on the approaching tank. With the main gun broken the only outward threat it held was sheer tonnage. The broken tread flapped and sounded like a thousand mice squealing in pain as it came around.

The snout of an assault rifle poked through one of the view ports. Near the mouth of the alley Alireza unshouldered one of the LAWs she'd recovered from the dead Russians. She snapped it open proficiently, extended the ends and flipped up the sights. Before the gunner inside the tank had a chance to fire, she squeezed the trigger.

The Executioner got a brief image of the 94 mm warhead leaving the rocket tube, then saw only the vapor trail it left. Backwash from the explosion rolled over him, and he maintained his feet with difficulty.

Evidently the collision with the building, the truck and the implosion that had ripped the turret gun away had weakened the cupola. When the LAW rocket impacted against the Chobham armor, the explosive sheered through the last of the retaining bolts. The turret flipped away and left the lower section of the tank bared and unprotected. It rocked to a stop.

Bolan closed the distance. When the warrior reached the two halves of the tank, Alireza was at his back. The three corpses inside were torn and bloody. No one was alive.

Bolan leathered the .44 and recovered his M-16 from the debris. He looked at the woman and said, "Thanks."

Her return gaze was cool. "I was just doing my job, Striker." She gave him her back as she walked across the street.

Bolan dropped his assault rifle into a ready position in both hands as he followed. He tapped the transmit button on the headset. "Eagle One."

"Go, Striker."

"The situation?"

"We've got a handle on it here, but it sounds like the rest of the city's going to hell in a handbasket."

"Have you contacted Desert Lightning Base?"

"As soon as you said to. I expect to see aerial movement from that quarter any second now."

Bolan cleared the frequency. "What about the attacks on Israel and Saudi Arabia?" he called to Alireza.

They were in the alley again before the woman answered. "Still ongoing," she replied.

Keeping the backtrack covered, Bolan calculated the attack scenario the Iraqis and the terrorist groups would most likely follow, then plotted interception efforts that would cut the assault off at the knees. The previous attacks had been highly successful. Kuwait City had almost been rendered defenseless and teetered on the edge of being consumed by the military might left over from the first Iraqi conflict.

He turned away from the grim thoughts. It wasn't time to pull the pin on Kuwait yet. There was still a lot of fight left in the country. After the carnage Iraqi troops had inflicted under Saddam Hussein, the Kuwaiti people would be less likely to pull out early. They knew from experience that abandoning their homes and throwing themselves on the mercy of others could be as dangerous as staying for the battle.

The Executioner intended to see that the grim avengers in the allied forces and the local population had the chance to stand hard against their aggressors.

2

Yakov Katzenelenbogen held his hands well above his head as the Israeli Mossad agents in plainclothes poured into the small apartment. Two of the younger men aimed Beretta 92-F 9 mm pistols at the Phoenix Force leader's midsection. Katz didn't try to move. They had him cold, and causing injury to them in a vain attempt to escape wasn't a viable option.

Three other men in plainclothes entered the room and went through the apartment, checking the closet and bathroom with practiced ease. The two men standing watch over Katz closed in, staying away from his right side and the wicked metal hook that served as his hand. Moving cautiously, knowing there was no real hurry because the Mossad agents wouldn't have time to stop him, Katz removed the ear-throat headset from his face and dropped it onto the hardwood floor.

"Wait!" one of the agents ordered.

Katz raised his hand again, then lifted his heel and crunched the headset beneath it. The rest of Phoenix Force knew he'd been taken captive and would change operating frequencies on the mission as a matter of course, but he wanted to keep the Mossad agents as much in the dark as possible.

The Israeli agent cursed in a low voice, then extended his pistol more forcibly. "Step back slowly. Do it now."

Katz complied. Out of habit he kept to one side of the shattered window at the other end of the room. Sofian Nejd's broken body still lay in the alleyway below. A cart driver stood nearby while his donkey shifted its feet in a bored fashion. Not even the smell of fresh blood was enough to unnerve the pack animal.

"Murderer!"

Katz looked back at the woman who addressed him.

She was lean and young, good-looking if not for the obvious rage that scarred her face. She was naked from the waist up, her breasts quivering with the emotion that gripped her. Her skirt was dark and ended just above the knee. Its disheveled appearance told of her scuffle with Katz, which had taken place only moments before as she'd tried to keep Nejd from going down under the Phoenix Force member's gun. Scratches bled crimson from her legs and arms. A trickle of blood marred the corner of her mouth.

One of the Mossad agents holstered his pistol long enough to shrug out of his jacket and give it to her.

She ignored it, brushed the arm out of her way and took a step toward Katz. Her eyes brimmed with tears. "He is a murderer," she said again. "He killed my husband. He broke into our home like a thief, then shoved poor Sofian through the window."

Katz didn't say anything. He was all too familiar with the intelligence machinery. The men before him were only there to assess the situation. He preferred to wait and deal with the people who made the decisions, provided he got the chance to talk to them. He had only false papers that could be easily seen through despite Aaron "Bear" Kurtzman's best efforts with Stony Man resources. And Barbara Price hadn't sanctioned the mission through the Mossad or Israeli government despite the fact that they were on the same side. Cutting to the bone, the Mossad had a right to shoot him down where he stood as a spy working against their country during a war situation.

The woman spit at him, and it hit Katz's chin. He wiped it away while one of the agents wrapped an arm around the woman and pulled her back. Another man forcibly put his jacket across her shoulders and ordered her to cover herself. Two of them guided her out of the apartment.

"Up against the wall," one of the agents ordered.

Katz turned, faced the wall and put his hands up high. He listened. There were no sounds of gunfire. He smiled because it meant David McCarter had managed to get the rest of the team clear of the area. They could resume following up on the terrorist cell they'd been assigned to track down and destroy.

A hand pressed into the small of the Phoenix Force leader's back and pinned him against the wall. He glanced out the window. Uniformed Israeli soldiers had surrounded Sofian Nejd's body and were cordoning off the area. Angry Palestinians shouted curses and threats that echoed hollowly inside the apartment. The woman's shrill voice joined them, then was silenced only seconds later.

"Take off the hook," the Israeli said.

Katz reached up, unlocked the hook from his prosthesis, then held it dangling from his fingertips.

"Drop it."

The hook clanged off the hardwood floor.

The second man frisked him with labored thoroughness. Katz took each discovered weapon from his mental catalog as it was taken away. He'd already given up his Beretta. The straight razor in his coat pocket went next, followed by the small lock-back penknife in his pant pocket. The Intratec Protec-25 .45 ACP in its ankle holster was quickly emptied. The extra magazines for the Beretta and the hideaway pistol were removed from his pockets and the shoulder rig. The gear made an impressive pile on the floor.

However, as thorough as the man had been, he'd missed the garrote sewn into the sleeve of Katz's jacket as well as the slender, flexible knife blade in the hem that could be joined with his belt buckle and rendered into a versatile stiletto.

"Turn around."

Katz complied.

Careful to stay out of his partner's line of fire, the second man turned down Katz's jacket so that it bound the Phoenix Force leader around the shoulders. A pair of handcuffs further restricted movement.

Static crackled over a walkie-talkie held by one of the agents. The man drew it closer to his ear, then looked up at the rest of the group. "We're under missile attack. Quick, secure this room."

Public-address systems mounted along the alleys below repeated the same information in Hebrew, Arabic, French, English, Japanese and German. The crowds gathered below dispersed. Two of the uniformed Israelis grabbed Nejd's body under the arms and dragged it to shelter. The cart driver whipped his donkey into a lively trot that scattered packages in the cart's wake.

Then the view through the window vanished, covered by a section of plastic wrap one of the agents found in the small kitchen. Strips of gray duct tape ripped free of the roll and were laid in overlapping lines along the plastic sheets.

More Mossad agents poured into the room, most of them already wearing gas masks and looking like underwater creatures out of their element. The door was shut. The majority of the newcomers helped to complete sealing the room. When the roll of tape played out, more were pulled out of attaché cases that had contained gas masks. Katz guessed that duct tape had become standard issue since the Iraqis had proved willing to attack Israel last year.

His stomach knotted when he thought of what would happen if the Scuds did carry poison gas or nuclear warheads. The possibility hadn't been far from his mind since the Arab terrorists had attacked the Olympic athletes in Barcelona, Spain, less than forty-eight hours earlier. Women and children weren't safe in a madman's war, and in a terrorist's bid for power, they were highly desirable pawns.

"Sit!" the Mossad agent ordered.

Katz sat, his back to the wall while the men huddled in the room with sick anticipation.

The first impacts were distant. Thunder rolled in from them, making the muted light seen through the sheets of plastic seem like something from a fantasy.

Only a few of the Mossad agents had radios. The rest listened intently.

The Scuds' detonations came closer, shaking the ground now with their approach. Katz's thoughts turned to McCarter and the rest of the team. He wondered if they'd had enough lead time to hole up, wondered if they would lose their other options to trail the terrorist cell.

The apartment shuddered under the bombardment. Vases spilled from the walls and smashed to fragments that spread across the floor. Dishes jostled from the shelving in the kitchen and went clattering across the countertops.

One of the agents, this one with a heavier build and slower movements denoting someone past his prime, pointed at Katz and growled an order. Another agent crossed the room, pulled a gas mask from a briefcase and fitted it around Katz's head.

Katz sneezed when the odor of the filters trickled into his nose. Everything looked blurred on the other side of the Plexiglas lenses. The building continued to shake. Then the bombing subsided. Minutes passed.

An agent ripped his gas mask from his head and sucked in a deep breath. He spoke into the walkie-talkie gripped in his hand, then looked up at the rest of the group. "There were no gas warheads," he reported. "Only explosives."

A collective sigh of relief passed inaudibly through the Mossad agents.

The gray-suited man who'd given the command to place the gas mask on Katz stepped in front of him. Reaching forward slowly enough so that no threat was offered, the man unfastened Katz's gas mask and removed it.

Cool air touched the Phoenix Force leader's perspiration-covered face. The brown eyes on the other side of the Plexiglas lenses seemed familiar. Red lines through the whites of the eyes were roadmaps of age and worry.

The man removed his own mask, revealed a head of bleached gray hair that showed an expanse of pink scalp beneath. Thick pouches of flesh the color of fresh bruises underlined his deep-set eyes. "Yakov," he said in a deep, sonorous voice.

"Elrad," Katz said, nodding a hello.

"It has been a long time, my friend."

"Yes." Elrad Morganstein had been a co-worker as well as a friend in the old days before Katz's wife had been killed under mysterious circumstances, before the warrior's heart and soul had persuaded him the missions generated from Stony Man Farm lay more in accordance with what he wanted for the world rather than the sometimes paranoia-influenced operations the Mossad was involved in.

Morganstein spread his hands and pursed his lips in displeasure. "When you left us, I was afraid it would come down to this some day. The world isn't as big as it once was."

"You know I'm no spy."

"I know you would voluntarily bring no ill will toward this country." Morganstein sighed. "But your goals are no longer our goals."

Emergency vehicle sirens screamed in the distance. The air raid horns shrilled an all-clear.

"Who are you working for, Yakov?" Morganstein fixed him with a steely stare.

"I can't say."

"You mean you won't."

"You know with me it is the same thing."

"The Americans knew of Sofian Nejd?"

Katz returned the other man's gaze full measure.

"How much do they know?" Morganstein asked softly.

Katz shook the chains just now snapped around his ankles. "I'm your prisoner. Jail me, release me or deport me."

"What of the American government? Won't it come to your rescue?"

"I don't know anyone in the American government."

"The CIA perhaps?"

Katz remained silent. If Morganstein wanted to think he was there at the behest of the CIA, it would keep the Mossad from looking for connections that would lead them to Stony Man Farm.

"It's suspected that you're working with one of the clandestine American agencies, Yakov. Save yourself some discomfort. Tell me what you know about Sofian Nejd and the terrorist cell he's affiliated with here."

"Nothing. He threw himself out the window and died before I was able to question him."

"And the woman?"

"Perhaps she knows something. I'm uncertain."

Morganstein stripped the plastic from the window. The pool of blood where Nejd had lain gleamed darkly, streaked where his bare feet had been dragged through it. "Things could have ended differently here if your people had agreed to work with the Mossad on this."

"You can't say that."

Morganstein faced him with a harsh look. "Yes, I can, Yakov. You've placed an entire country under an executioner's ax wielded by that Iraqi psychopath."

With effort Katz kept his face bland. He was fairly certain Morganstein didn't mean the hateful words, but they still stung. Just as he was sure the Mossad agent had intended them to. Honest anger was at their root. Israel saw itself at war with the rest of the world in one form or another. That line of thinking had saved them a number of times, but it just as readily held them back from the peace her people desired, as well.

"Get him out of here." Morganstein turned away and leaned against the window to look out over the city. "But leave him healthy and whole. I'll speak to him later."

"Yes, sir."

The two agents propelled Katz toward the door again. He went as quickly as the leg irons would permit, nearly falling once when his captors shoved him through the door.

Outside, the air still crackled with the noises filling the void left by the exploding Scud missiles. Sirens and Klaxons whined and screamed alternately. Below the third-floor landing groups of people had filled the narrow street again. Their voices stopped for an instant, then continued when they noticed Katz sandwiched between the two plainclothes agents.

Two streets later, followed by a crowd that continued to shout questions at the plainclothesmen in Hebrew and Arabic, Katz was shoved into the back seat of an unmarked subcompact car. A glance let him know the handles had been stripped from the doors. Wire mesh separated him from the front seat. He had to struggle to regain a seated position.

The crowd swarmed up around the vehicle, waving angry fists at both the Mossad agents and Katz. The Phoenix Force leader surveyed them. None were familiar from the

files Barbara Price and Kurtzman had assembled of the
known terrorists operating out of the West Bank.

A few moments later a dozen uniformed Israeli troops
forced their way down the street on foot. They formed a
flying wedge in the crowd with flashing police batons and
rifle butts.

The crowd, primarily Arab, surged forward, challenging
the soldiers' authority with loud voices and threats.

Without hesitation the commanding officer of the unit
opened fire with his assault rifle. Three Arabs went down
immediately. After that there were no more problems getting the car under way.

Katz watched the soldiers drag the bodies to the sidewalk
in the car's rearview mirror.

CARL "IRONMAN" LYONS glanced at his watch. It was 6:22
a.m. The sun over Brooklyn had been trying to break
through the eastern wall of thunderheads for almost an hour
now. The second hand started its sweep of the last minute.
Rosario "Politician" Blancanales, Leo Turrin and Her-
mann "Gadgets" Schwarz should be in place now.

Dressed in black jeans, a dark blue windbreaker, joggers
and a black turtleneck with a black New York Yankees ball
cap covering his blond hair, he knew he blended in with the
long shadows draping the apartment building behind him.

He took up the specially silenced Marlin 70HC that sat
canted against the steel framework of the sixth-story landing, checked the action and blew imaginary dust from the
ejector. The 25-round clip twisted awkwardly from beneath
the five-pound weapon.

Lyons smiled when he remembered John "Cowboy"
Kissinger's assessment of the rifle. The Stony Man wea-
ponsmith had called it a varmint gun, and the big Able
Team warrior hadn't disagreed.

With the 22LR rounds traveling faster than the speed of sound, they'd create a wake of audibles that couldn't be muffled. But the round also offered quick efficiency on follow-up shots by being nearly recoilless.

Other weapons of war hung from his body. The colt Python .357 was snugged securely in shoulder leather. A military-styled holster held a Government Model Colt .45. A PANCOR Corporation Jackhammer 12-gauge battle shotgun lay at his feet, its shoulder sling coiled for instant access. Extra magazines and the disposable cylinders for the Jackhammer filled ammo pouches at his waist.

He took a deep breath and settled into the heft of the Marlin as he brought up his first target. He used open sights. A scope would have been too limiting for the field of view he was expected to cover in so short a time. There were four targets up here waiting on him. The rest of the Able Team and Turrin, coming up from the lower levels, would have their hands full once the terrorists knew their nest had been discovered. It was important that he take out as many of them as he could.

The location had been given to them a few hours earlier. The decision had been made not to include New York's Finest, which would undoubtedly count against them politically when the operation came under public scrutiny. But as the major processor of the false passports and identities the terrorists in the United States were traveling under, Able Team had elected to take the hardsite down themselves. There would be no confusion over Miranda rights. The terrorists would be given a choice between living or dying.

All four guards were in view when Lyons took up the slack on the rifle's trigger. Two men ran low, maintaining the integrity of the fifth-floor perimeters. The other two covered the windows from the sixth and seventh floors.

Between them a two-lane street ran through the outer perimeters of Brooklyn before tying up with Prospect Park

West. Traffic had already started to choke the street in both directions.

Making himself as much a part of the building as he could, Lyons aimed for the center of his first target's face and fired four times in rapid succession. The terrorist spun away, blood covering his features as he crashed blindly through a plate-glass window near the landing.

Already on the move, Lyons picked up his second target and zipped three precise rounds into the man's heart. A bullet slammed into the metalwork above the blond Able Team warrior.

Lyons found target number three lying prone in a window and searching for him through a scope. He instinctively focused on the flash of light from the sniper scope that came from the center of the man's face, then squeezed the trigger five times. The flash of light went away. The gunner slumped forward with his hands hanging out.

The fourth man was still fumbling for his rifle when Lyons's bullets drilled into the exposed portion of his throat and drove him backward.

Abandoning the Marlin, Lyons took up the grappling hook/compressed airgun combination. The recoil from the released compressed air shoved him backward. He rolled with the force and watched with satisfaction as the grappling hook smacked into the sixth-floor landing, trailing the thin cable.

He secured his end of the cable above his head, then clamped on a tracked handwheel. Donning a pair of gloves, he attached a safety line to his combat rigging, then leaped out over the street and sped down the incline toward the other building. He hit the button on his ear-throat headset, cutting into the frequency Able Team was using for the mission. "This is Ironman. I'm airborne."

"Roger, Ironman," Schwarz radioed back. "Sticker's on his way. Pol and I have set up a hell of a reception for the early birds."

The cable bowed slightly in the middle, slowed a little, but continued an incline that kept Lyons going. Schwarz cleared the frequency. For a moment Lyons thought he was going to make ground zero on the sixth floor with no problems.

Then he saw his second target shift and come up with an assault rifle. He stared down the barrel, knowing there was nowhere to run.

3

Autofire sparked from the handwheel over Lyons's head, vibrating the tight cable. He released his hold on the hand-grips and hoped like hell the safety harness would take his weight. If the incline had been steeper, he would have trusted his speed alone to be his defense.

The street spun dizzyingly below him. Cars whished by, their normal noises punctuated by horn blasts.

He found the PANCOR Jackhammer by feel. Shaking the sling loose from his shoulders, the safety harness linked to his combat webbing causing some difficulty, he brought up the 12 gauge shotgun. He flicked the fire selector to auto-matic and cut loose a 3-round burst of double-aught buck that shattered bricks and struck fire from the metal cage near his target.

The terrorist was thrown up against the wall beside the window, then spilled over the side of the landing. The re-coil from the combat shotgun twisted Lyons violently and caused the safety harness straps to seize up around his chest. He flailed upward as he spun helplessly, then stalled in his forward momentum. His hand closed around the hand unit attached to the cable. With an effort that felt as if it nearly ripped his shoulder from the socket, he halted his spin. A tug forward on the cable got him under way again.

"Ironman."

Lyons tapped the transmit button on his headset. "Go, Sticker."

Sticker was Leo Turrin's code name. The stocky little Fed had accompanied Able Team north from Stony Man Farm to help track down the terrorist processing center.

"What's your status?" Turrin asked.

Lyons glanced around the small living room he'd broken into. The sofa and mismatched chairs looked as if they'd come from a garage sale. The smell inside the room was stale, covered over by the odor of pungent spices. "I'm intact," Lyons reported.

"I caught your near-swan dive and wondered if you'd ran into any more trouble."

A terrorist bolted from hiding in the hallway leading back to the bedroom. Lyons went down behind the moth-eaten couch and raised the Jackhammer.

Reports from the terrorist's handgun echoed within the room. Bits of material and hunks of padding showered across the Able Team warrior from the bullets that tore through the back of the sofa.

Rolling, Lyons came up on his knees, weapon tracking. A double charge of buckshot caught the terrorist in the chest and slammed him through the door of the hallway closet.

Lyons got to his feet and swiveled his head to take in the perimeters. No one else appeared to be in the room. Cordite smoke turned the darkness of the room to a swirling charcoal-gray. He tapped the transmit button. "Sticker. Status?"

"On the move," Turrin replied.

"Pol?"

"Here, Ironman." Blancanales sounded out of breath.

Lyons opened the door. Bullets ripped through the wooden panels and blew long splinters over him. He ducked back inside. At least three men were in the hallway. "Gadgets?"

"Leave me alone for a minute. I got some business to tend to." Gunfire, up close and personal, was transmitted along the communications frequency.

Nudging the fire selector back up to full-auto, Lyons swung back into the hallway. Just as he jerked the big shotgun up to his shoulder, he saw one of the terrorists lob something at him from the other end of the hall. He tracked it instinctively, recognized it as a grenade and fired. At least one of the shotgun blasts hit the grenade and bounced it off the ceiling back in the direction it had come.

The concussive force the bomb expended a moment later pushed at the loose folds of Lyons's windbreaker. Walls went down on both sides of the hall, lying open at least three other rooms on the floor. The building was old, next door to being condemned, but Lyons was sure the terrorist cell had paid their Mafia connection dearly for the privilege of staying there.

He shucked the empty magazine cylinder from the Jackhammer and slipped a fresh one into place. Automatically counting down in his head from the time he'd burst into the room, he charged out into the hallway. The numbers on this operation were running thin. Provided the terrorist cell had computerized access to Social Security, State Department, and Department of Motor Vehicle files, it still wouldn't take long to destroy the evidence.

He reached the end of the hall, alerted by the glimmer of movement from the upper staircase. Bullets bounced painfully from the Kevlar Second Chance armor he wore under his jacket and turtleneck. He swept the Jackhammer up, squeezed the trigger, then stepped over the sprawled corpse on his way to the seventh floor.

"Politician here. First floor's clean, guys."

Lyons keyed the transmitter. "Fifth floor's likewise."

Police sirens keened in the background, trickling in through the partially raised dirt-smudged windows that blunted what little morning sunlight existed.

At the top of the staircase Lyons was forced to ground by a withering burst of gunfire from a pair of Uzis held by two terrorists. Stretched out prone on the wooden floor, he held on to the combat shotgun and kept the trigger down. Six loads of double-aught cleared the hallway.

Within less than a minute Lyons ascertained that the sixth floor was clean, as well. He was on his way back down the staircase when he alerted the rest of the team. His breath came in heaving gasps, ribs bruised from the bullet impacts and the frantic pace he was putting his body through.

"Bingo," Turrin called softly. "This is Sticker."

"Where?" Lyons asked, knowing his impatience could be heard in his tone.

The police sirens were closer now. A glance out a landing window showed three NYPD units screeching to a halt in front of the building.

"Fourth floor," Turrin replied.

"Gadgets."

"On my way, Ironman. Just hold your water till I get there."

The building suddenly shuddered.

"What the hell was that?" Lyons asked.

"Somebody tried to take the elevator down," Blancanales said. "Told you me and Gadgets had some nasty surprises on tap for these guys."

"Yeah, well, before you break your arm patting yourself on the back for being so goddamn efficient, you might want to remember we could use a couple of these people alive to answer some questions." Lyons dropped onto the fourth-floor landing.

Three terrorists wheeled around the corner and appeared just as surprised to see him as he was to see them. Unable to bring the Jackhammer into effective play, he used his momentum and the element of surprise that was his. Yelling, he threw himself at the terrorists before they could fire or retreat. His spread-out arms took them all down in a heap.

He smashed his forehead into the face of the terrorist under him as the guy struggled to aim the pistol in his hand. The gun went off, and though the bullet was wide of the mark, the muzzle-flash burned Lyons's cheek.

Forcing himself to his knees, Lyons caught another man in the throat with the yoke of his hand and crushed his windpipe. The terrorist fell to one side and started gagging on his own blood. Catching the Jackhammer up, he swung the butt around hard enough to break the third man's jaw. Bone crunched and teeth shattered. Once he was on his feet, he kicked the first man into unconsciousness.

On the fourth floor he turned into the corridor with the shotgun held at waist level. Two more terrorists stood in front of the open elevator doors. No cage waited inside, and they stared down into the dark depths.

Two more men stood to either side of a room in the middle of the hallway on the right. Recognizing the plastic explosives on their hands, Lyons opened fire without hesitation. The shotgun blasts blew them away at once but drew the fire of the other men in front of the elevator.

Lyons dodged back into the stairwell. Glass from one of the loosely hung double doors exploded in fragments that sliced his face. He drew the Government Colt and stretched around the corner.

Turrin stepped into view, shouldering a CAR-15 assault rifle. The Fed looked like something out of an Italian spaghetti western with his duster blowing loose around him, but his handling of the rifle would have left those cowboys in the dust.

Lyons squeezed the trigger of the .45, and the bodies of the two terrorists tumbled over into the empty elevator shaft.

Turrin raced for the plastic explosives lying in the corridor and caught the charge with the side of his foot. The C-4 dropped into the elevator shaft after the terrorists. Less than fifteen seconds later the plastic went off in a burst that scattered roiling flames from the elevator shaft.

"Son of a bitch," Lyons said as he came to a stop outside the doors of the room the terrorists had been preparing to destroy. "I didn't think they'd had time to arm that goddamn thing."

Turrin tightened his grip on the CAR-15. "You think I'd have made a grandstand play like that if I'd thought they had? I just didn't want to take any chances."

Lyons lifted the Jackhammer and nodded at Turrin. The Able Team warrior went through the door first with the combat shotgun on selective fire, Turrin on his heels.

The room was free of terrorists.

Lyons hit the transmit button on his headset. "Where are you, Gadgets?"

"Coming. That's me breathing down your neck."

The room was filled with desks containing computer equipment and telephones. Whoever had hacked through the wall on the south side to enlarge the room had done a lousy job. Thin runners of wallpapered Sheetrock clung to the two-by-fours cutting through the middle of the double room.

Lyons glanced through the window, catching sight of a guy in the building across the street with SWAT stenciled in yellow letters across his back. He grabbed the string and lowered the blinds, shutting out the whirling red cherries scattered across the front of the apartment building. "Pol?"

"I'm covering the back door."

"Affirmative, guy, but you got friendlies about to crawl all over you."

"I've already noticed them."

"Damn!" Turrin exclaimed from across the room.

Lyons looked at the Fed. Turrin held up a fistful of blank documents carrying official seals. "They had a regular factory going on here. Birth certificates, Social Security, I-9s, W-4s. The works, man." He slapped the side of the camera in the corner of the room in disgust. "Even had one-day processing on pictures. Christ, what a setup."

Schwarz ran into the room carrying a heavy duffel bag slung over one shoulder. He started to work without preamble. The contents of the pack were scattered over a table that he cleared with one sweep of his arm. Lyons could identify some of the computer equipment, but not all of it. He'd had trouble keeping up with technological improvements back during his days on the Los Angeles Police Department. Young as he'd been then, he'd adopted the old ways of professional manhunters.

"Leo," Schwarz said as he tucked a small multibit screwdriver behind one ear, "you want to get me a line to the Farm?"

Turrin picked up one of the nearby phones and dialed.

Lyons palmed another receiver and punched up another line.

"What are you doing?" Turrin asked.

"Buying us some time." Lyons placed a forefinger against the blinds and watched as another SWAT van pulled onto the scene. He had no doubt that the buildings would be crawling with sharpshooters within minutes. He dialed 911, got a dispatcher and reported a police emergency, knowing they'd already have his number and know he was calling from inside the building. Then he told the dispatch officers he was holding hostages and had the building rigged to explode. He hung up before the guy could ask questions.

"That was a really lousy Arab accent," Blancanales said from the doorway.

"It'll work," Lyons said. "Glad to see you could join us."

"Tracked down a couple of stragglers," Blancanales told him. "I know how you hate to leave loose ends."

Through the slitted blinds Lyons saw the front line of police blues sag back to the parked vehicles. More cops fanned out behind their patrol units and started setting up roadblocks to keep the gathering crowd back. Traffic was blocked at both ends of the street.

"They won't stay out there sitting on their thumbs for long," Turrin said. He had a police band radio in his hand with a plug jacked into his ear. "They already figure they're seeing the tip of another Iraqi terrorist operation."

Lyons glanced at Schwarz. Most of the components the man had brought in his pack seemed to be operational. "How long?"

"Till it gets done. You bought us time. Let me get on with my job." Schwarz seated himself behind one of the computer boards and started hitting the keys. After a few hesitant starts, he started a constant clatter, then reached for the phone Turrin held out to him. Cradling it on a modem pad, he watched as rows of data entries scrolled by on the monitor. "I got a core dump going now. Bear'll have everything they've got in memory in just a few minutes."

"Any interesting tidbits turn up?" Lyons asked.

"Couldn't tell you. I went for the heart of the thing and reduced it all to machine language. You'll have to wait on Barb and Aaron for the translations."

Lyons tried to make himself be patient. It was difficult. All he could think of while the hard disk clunked through its electronic information was the number of innocents that had died in terrorist attacks within the United States. He'd witnessed one of them himself and seen the others played back while at the debriefing at Stony Man Farm.

The computer files Schwarz was accessing might contain the names and false identities of every terrorist who had been slipped into the country during the past year. Every last one of them would be tracked down, if he had to do it himself. And that was a promise the big man fully intended to keep.

DAVID MCCARTER SLID DOWN the stair railing and landed on his feet, running. People in his path took one look at his hard-featured face and got out of the way. Angry, fearful shouts punctuated the din of police and emergency vehicle sirens and the all-clear signal being blared out by the Klaxons.

He drew only a little attention from the people thronging the streets. After the Scud missiles, a fox-faced man with longish hair wearing blue jeans, boots, a chambray work shirt and a lightweight jacket could only command so much notice. He didn't mind. Even an unpracticed eye might have noticed the Browning Hi-Power tucked under his left arm. He'd abandoned the Galil sniping rifle atop the building he'd just left. Images of Katz being unceremoniously dumped into the Mossad vehicle kept roaming through his mind.

He clung to the edges of the alley and still managed a decent clip in spite of the people gathered there. Tapping the transmit button on his ear-throat headset, he said, "Phoenix Five, this is Phoenix Two. Come in, mate."

Calvin James answered immediately. "Go, Phoenix Two."

"You've seen the situation regarding Phoenix One?"

"Affirmative. How do you want to play this? Phoenix One left instructions that we were to proceed with the mission in any event."

"Call me old-fashioned," McCarter said, "but I always leave with the one who brought me to the dance."

"Understood. But you're dealing with the Mossad. Phoenix One might have some strings he can pull even if we leave him in place."

"String-pulling takes time, laddie, and we're running kind of thin on that resource. Me, I prefer to keep the whole unit operational. And trusting political games with this current state of affairs seems a lot like sticking your hand into a viper's hole and hoping you don't get bitten."

"So what's the agenda?"

McCarter cut across an open area and dashed to the parked Honda Civic in the small parking area just off the street Katz's captors were traveling. "You blokes find our secondary target and discover whatever you can. I'll either have Phoenix One back safe and secure in time to move with you, or you'll be looking for a couple of more players."

"You figured out how you're going to do that yet?"

McCarter grinned at his reflection in the rearview mirror as he keyed the Civic to life. "Negative, Phoenix Two. But I've always been a man who likes a little uncertain adventure to spice things up. Good hunting. Phoenix Two out."

"Good hunting to you, too, buddy. Phoenix Five out."

Shifting smoothly, McCarter pulled the car up through the swell of traffic and trailed in the wake of the Mossad vehicle. Katz was going to be angry when he found out, and McCarter knew it. But it wasn't as if he was risking the mission. So far they were hunting up leads, and three men could do that just as easily as four. And the way McCarter had it figured, Katz wouldn't have anything to complain about unless he got caught, too.

Which, McCarter thought as he gazed at the Mossad vehicle three cars ahead of him, was all the more reason not to get snared.

"STONY MAN BASE, this is Stony Man One. Do you read? Over."

"Stony One, you have Stony Base. Go ahead. Over."

Mack Bolan surveyed the western perimeters around Kuwait City with wide-angle binoculars from the copilot seat of the AH-1S HueyCobra Jack Grimaldi piloted. North of the city a ragged line of Iraqi tanks rolled across the desert hills on a collision course with civilization. Smoke still spiraled up from various attack sites hit by the Scuds. A convoy of A-6 Intruders and A-10 Thunderbolt IIs were in flight to intercept the tanks. Several of the turret guns opened up and lobbed a salvo of shells at the city less than three miles away.

In quick, terse terms the warrior sketched the meeting he'd had with Talia Alireza less than half an hour ago, emphasizing the presence of Russian agents. He waved to Grimaldi. The pilot nodded and fell into attack formation with the rest of the aerial unit that allied forces had been able to field against the attacking tanks.

Barbara Price listened at the other end of the specially scrambled satellite transmission without comment.

"We got company calling," Grimaldi said from higher up.

Bolan followed the pilot's pointing finger and ID'ed the specks growing closer in the soft blue of the sky. He nodded his comprehension to Grimaldi, jerked a thumb upward to let his comrade-in-arms know to extend the HueyCobra's ceiling over the battle zone, then turned his attention back to Barbara Price.

"You're saying operations somewhere at this end have been compromised," Price responded. "Over."

"That's affirmative, Stony Base. Contact between Striker and Valkyrie was mapped and preplotted before it took place. Over." Bolan gave the Striker code name a separate identity. As Colonel Rance Pollock, he was in charge of U.S. forces in the gulf confrontation, with presidential backing pipelined straight in from the White House. As Striker, he was head of a covert U.S. force willing to operate behind Iraqi lines with orders to terminate terrorist and Iraqi aggression with whatever means possible. Provided someone had managed to tap the Stony Man computers in some fashion, observance of records would lead their intelligence circles to believe Pollock and Striker were two different people.

The allied aerial forces pulled up slightly. Some of them went into inclines to match altitudes with the approaching jets.

"They're Iraqi," Grimaldi called out. "You got MiGs and Mirage F-1s on a direct heading to us."

"Hold on, Stony Base. Over," Bolan said.

"Stony Base standing by. Over."

Bolan flipped over to the main com/net linking the allied forces. "Azure Typhoon Leader, this is Scarlet Leader One. Over."

"Scarlet Leader One, you have Azure Typhoon Leader. Over."

"Roger, Azure Typhoon Leader. You are to intercept and shoot down the approaching forces on your mark. Repeat, you are to engage and destroy under your orders. Scarlet Leader One will be standing by. When you are given the signal to get your people out of that area, you will disengage and do so immediately. Over."

"That's affirmative, Scarlet Leader One. Azure Typhoon Leader out."

Bolan clicked to another band, punching in the Desert Lightning troop frequency. Azure Typhoon force was a small aerial contingent from the decks of the USS *Theodore Roosevelt,* Azure Typhoon Base. More F-14 Tomcats were en route as they were brought on-line, but they would be minutes in getting to the site. And those were minutes the battle for Kuwait City didn't have.

"Desert Lightning Two, this is Desert Lightning One. Over."

"Desert Lightning One, you have Desert Lightning Two. Over." Lieutenant Colonel Joshua Eldridge's voice sounded tense and strained.

Bolan wrote it off partly as the tension created by the forging of their forced and unexpected relationship. At another time he knew they might have found a common meeting ground that would have allowed them the luxury of friendship as well as places in command. "What is your twenty, Two? Over." He unfolded a terrain map from the case that never left his side.

Without warning the HueyCobra heeled over. Machine gun fire flared from the battle copter's tail briefly before Grimaldi got them above it. "Ack-ack guns from the tanks," the Stony Man pilot said, referring to the 12.7 mm antiaircraft guns on the Russian-made MBTs.

Eldridge gave the location of the Desert Lightning contingent, using the grid names they'd set up shortly after Bolan had joined the unit.

Bolan vectored in on the Desert Lightning position, then keyed the transmit button again. "Desert Lightning Two, set up the MLRS. Switch your frequency over to the com/net. You have two minutes to fire on my signal. Over."

"Affirmative, Desert Lightning One. Two out."

Flicking the frequency back to the main com/net, Bolan hit the transmit button. "Azure Typhoon Base, this is Scarlet Leader One. Over."

"Go, Scarlet Leader, you have Azure Typhoon Base. Over."

Scanning his map, the Executioner substituted the Desert Lightning configurations and call signals for the Navy's. The admiral was quick to respond, belaying orders immediately for the battleship USS *Missouri* to ready guns and Cruise missiles.

The air in front of the HueyCobra seemed filled with streaking hornet shapes. Black plumes of smoke trailed fallen aircraft to fiery impacts against the desert sand.

"On my signal, Azure Typhoon Base," Bolan said. "Over."

"Aye, lad," the gruff old man said, "and good luck to you and your people. Azure Typhoon Base standing by. Over."

"Scarlet Leader One, this is Home Plate. Over."

"I read you, Home Plate. Over."

"Permission to advance against the tank line, sir. Over."

"Permission denied, Home Plate. Over." Bolan continued to survey the battle zone through his binoculars. Grimaldi was jockeying the HueyCobra around mercilessly. Triggering rounds from the rear weapon controls, the pilot had accounted for two of the tanks himself. Scars decorated the Plexiglas nose of the chopper and attested to Grimaldi's proximity to the battle.

"But, sir, that armor's going to be here in minutes."

"Denied, Home Plate," Bolan repeated. "Clear the frequency, mister. Over."

Home Plate cleared.

The HueyCobra shimmied when Grimaldi opened up the 20 mm turret guns. The heavy rounds raked the armored hides of the Russian tanks below and spilled human operators from the antiaircraft guns. Then they were past them, winging on for more open sky before going for another run.

Without warning a MiG-29 flashed by them, throttling back as it came screaming around.

Bolan tapped the transmitter. "Desert Lightning Two, this is Scarlet Leader One. Over."

"Copy, Scarlet Leader One. You have Two. Go ahead. Over."

"Are you set up there? Over."

"That's affirmative, Scarlet Leader One. Over."

"Azure Typhoon Leader, this is Scarlet Leader One. Over."

"Go, Scarlet Leader. Over."

"Break off the engagement, Azure. You and your men need to be a flock of screaming eagles headed for home at near-ground zero now. Over."

"Affirmative, Scarlet Leader. Azure Typhoon Leader out."

Grimaldi jerked the HueyCobra around and lined up to meet the latest pass of the MiG-29 that had singled them out. "Come on, you cocky bastard," the pilot said in a still, dry voice.

Bolan shifted his view away from the approaching MiG. Either Grimaldi had the attack craft or he didn't. The Executioner knew he was personally out of the play. He scanned the skies with his binoculars and saw the allied forces break off the aerial engagement. The Iraqi air force lagged behind them, obviously taken off guard by the surprising tactics.

Hitting the transmit button, feeling the attack chopper release twin Hellfire missiles that rocketed toward the charging MiG-29, Bolan said, "Desert Lightning Two, fire all twelve. Repeat, fire all twelve. Over."

"Affirmative, Scarlet Leader One. Two out."

"Azure Typhoon Base, you have the helm. Hope we have your ducks all in a row. Scarlet Leader One out."

The Hellfire missiles locked onto the Iraqi MiG. Unable to avoid them, the jet went nova and rained down over the desert sand.

"Get us the hell out of here, Jack," Bolan said. "This part of the desert's about to become scorched earth." He changed frequencies, picked up Stony Man Base again and hoped everything worked out as he'd planned.

FROM THE PASSENGER SEAT of his command jeep Lieutenant Colonel Eldridge watched the Multiple Launch Rocket System empty itself of all twelve deathbirds in just under a minute. He was a tall, blocky man with hands as big as spades. His gray hair looked darker because perspiration had matted it to his head. He shielded his china-blue eyes from the burning sand.

Pollock had called a daring plan; he had to give the man that even as much as he disliked him.

The armored vehicle holding the MLRS shuddered beneath the rapid launches. Despite being built on the same chassis as the M2 Bradley Infantry Fighting Vehicle and weighing some twenty-five tons, that kind of launching took its toll on machinery.

Eldridge took a pair of binoculars from his driver and trailed the streams of smoke through the air. Over seven thousand pounds of explosives were on their way across Kuwait City and the reforming air contingent that had challenged the invading Iraqi forces.

Then they were gone from sight.

He started to lower the field glasses, then noticed the silhouette of a man standing out in the center of the desert incline the Desert Lightning unit had started to advance on before Pollock's orders had come through. His heart leaped to his throat when he increased the powered magnification. The tiny servos whined as the lenses focused and reimaged.

It was definitely a man.

Lean and brown, his face concealed by shadows that shouldn't have existed under the blazing sun, the man stood unconcernedly at the top of the incline. Brown robes covered him from neck to toes.

Eldridge knew who it was without seeing the features. A cold chill seeped through him and collected along his spine. He gritted his teeth to keep them from chattering.

The man's name was Paul, and over twenty-six hours ago Eldridge had seen him die at the hands of the enemy, hung upside down from a flagpole with blood and fluids pouring from his body. His brief conversation with the young private had dredged up old feelings he'd forgotten he'd ever had.

The top of Paul's head held a glow. The shadows masking his features evaporated. He looked peaceful.

Eldridge couldn't take his eyes away from the dead man. Despite what he knew to be true, he was certain that was no corpse perched on top of the hill.

Paul spoke in a voice as soft and still as a summer night. "Joshua, He's waiting on you. There are many challenges ahead of you, but if you remember He is with you, you will overcome them. It is the time of the Beast, Joshua, just as you have been told all your life. You will know the Beast. You will know him from the prophecies because he will bear the mark upon his forehead."

Eldridge trembled. The voice sounded in some ways like his father's had on the better nights of the tent revivals he remembered so well. Those memories had been shut away so long, kept under mental lock and key until last year's war.

"Come," Paul said in that deathly still voice, "walk with me. We have much to talk about, and there still remains many preparations to make."

Unable to keep his eyes focused so intently anymore, Eldridge blinked. When his vision cleared, Paul was gone. So was the chill. He felt worn and clammy in his BDUs. The binoculars suddenly felt too heavy, so he dropped his arms to rest on the upraised window of the jeep.

"Sir? Are you all right, Colonel?"

Eldridge looked down at the corporal driving his jeep. It took him a handful of seconds to comprehend the question. Forcing himself into motion, he dropped into the passenger seat and shoved the binoculars into the glove compartment. "I'm perfectly fine, Corporal."

"Yes, sir. I just wondered because you seemed to—"

Making his voice boot-camp harsh, Eldridge said, "Get this vehicle in gear now, mister."

"Yes, sir!"

The jeep lunged forward. Eldridge slipped his M-16 from the rear deck and held it tightly across his lap. His groin felt tight and shriveled up, as if the chill still gripped him.

He glanced toward the incline and recoiled momentarily from the sun. There was nothing there now. But there had been. He was sure of it. And he feared it perhaps more than he reveled in the possibility of its existence.

Words drifted into his mind. It was from Revelation 13:7. "And it was given unto him to make war with the saints, and to overcome them: and power was given him over all kindreds, and tongues, and nations." It wasn't until he caught the sidelong glance from the corporal as they bounced up the hill that he realized he'd spoken the passage aloud.

4

The rockets from the Desert Lightning unit's MLRS came screaming into the battle zone. As they reached the target area, the black powder charges in the centers of the warheads exploded and scattered antiarmor mines, antipersonnel submunitions and bits of the polyurethane containers they'd been packed in over the approaching tanks.

Mack Bolan watched in professional satisfaction. The submunitions had cleared the allied aerial arm by nearly a mile. Some of the Iraqi forces beginning to follow the allied fighter jets into Kuwait City weren't so lucky.

The treadbusters and antipersonnel submunitions covered a space the size of four football fields. For a while that space included the heights. Nearly eight thousand deadly little packets covered the sky, dropped earthward suspended by ribbon parachutes.

A number of them impacted against the Iraqi fighters and blew the aircraft from the air. Bolan watched a MiG-21 take a round in the left wing, then come spiraling down in a haze of black smoke from an electrical fire.

The treadbusters scattered across and just a little ahead of the advancing line of tanks, making the way treacherous. Treads blew when they hit the antiarmor mines and stalled almost two dozen tanks immediately. The rest of the heavy cavalry broke the momentum they'd gained and came to an uncertain stop.

"Stony One, this is Stone Base. Over."

Bolan keyed the transmit button. "Stony Base, you have Stony One. Continuing our discussion concerning possible infiltration of our electronic intelligence relay stations, I'm advising we begin checking the home ground first. All incoming and outgoing communications should be routed through secondary alternatives to prevent any more possible tactical leakage. Over."

"Roger, Stony One, but it's also possible your leakage might be stemming from Valkyrie. Over."

The HueyCobra gained altitude in a jump under Grimaldi's practiced hands and swung out wide over Kuwait City as it came around to reform with the rest of Azure Typhoon Unit's low-flying contingent.

A dust storm, created by the exploding submunitions in the northern desert, swept in over the city's perimeters. Bolan saw no signs of life in the streets. Civilians had been ordered to shelter nearly an hour ago when the Scud shelling began.

"For the moment, Stony Base, I'm willing to give Valkyrie the benefit of the doubt. Valkyrie's intelligence regarding Desert Lightning and Kuwaiti defenses has been extremely limited. No way could Valkyrie have helped prepare for the assault we're facing here. And Valkyrie's unit has been engaged under heavy fire. This doesn't scan as a suicide play. You're advised to check out the Soviet sphere of influence first. As noted, we've encountered their players here. And so has Valkyrie. Over."

"Affirmative, Stony One, but you're going to be left on your own regarding covert intelligence over there. Over."

Bolan could tell by Barbara Price's tone that the Stony Man mission controller wasn't happy with the situation. She couldn't do her job effectively while working in the dark. "Understood, Stony Base. If anything comes up that can't wait, hard-wire it over and bypass the software. We can acquire some military channels to run Stony operations through if necessary. Over."

"Affirmative. I've already started the paperwork to push those channels through. You'll be notified as soon as we have them. Over."

Bolan took stock of the allied aerial teams. The American, British, Saudi, French and Kuwaiti jet fighters lanced out to reengage the Iraqi forces. The tank units were still stalled, mired in the maze of mines. More explosions ruptured under their treads and blew them loose.

"Understood, Stony Base. You people stay hard there. Stony One out."

"Good luck, Stony One. Stony Base out."

Bolan clicked back over to the main com/net, meshing smoothly mentally with the combat control stemming from Azure Typhoon Leader.

"Scarlet Leader One," the admiral at Azure Typhoon Base called, "be advised that the ground area there is critical fifteen seconds from this . . . mark. *Missouri* sends her best. Over."

"Roger, Azure Typhoon Base. Scarlet Leader One is advised. Express our appreciation to *Missouri*. Over."

"They'll be happy to hear that, Scarlet Leader One. The Chickenhawk unit you requested is on course and less than a minute behind *Missouri*'s love note. Azure Typhoon Base out."

"I have the guns, Jack," Bolan said as he dropped his hands over the HueyCobra's weapon control systems. "Get us in there where we can make a difference. It's time to root hog or die."

"Gotcha, Sarge." Under Grimaldi's direction the attack chopper kicked in the eighteen-hundred-horsepower turboshaft and flitted for the aerial battle commencing over the desert. With the pilot solely concerned with flying, the HueyCobra became a knife blade streaking through the sky.

Bolan got a missile lock on an Iraqi Mirage F-1. When he had a good ping, he released a Hellfire missile. With the "fire and forget" capability produced by the laser guidance system, the Executioner didn't bother to track the death-bird's progress. Out of the periphery of his vision he saw the fireball created by the Mirage's disappearance. A quick scan showed there were five Hellfires left. He swung the nose turret around, tracked an Iraqi MiG and squeezed the trigger of the 20 mm gun. The recoil vibrated the chopper's nose. Tracer fire glowed in the cross hairs, then the rounds punched holes in the jet's fuselage. It heeled over like a broken kite and lost altitude rapidly.

Keying the com/net, Bolan said, "Azure Typhoon Leader, this is Scarlet Leader One. Did you copy Azure Typhoon Base's transmission? Over."

"That's affirmative, Scarlet Leader One. Azure Typhoon Leader out."

Reacting immediately, Bolan stitched a line of 20 mm rounds through the Plexiglas canopy of another Iraqi fighter. In the distance and at the incredible speeds they were capable of, the jets looked like a swarm of mosquitoes, except for the black streams of smoke and the explosions.

The Executioner knew the engagement was going to be costly. There was no way around it. Allied defenses around Kuwait City were at a disadvantage. They'd been cut down during the restless period of peace following the previous year's war with Iraq. And the terrorist aggressions against the Kuwaiti defensive areas had taken a definite toll. Besides the barracks and the major airfield, the allies had lost the hospital, tons of equipment, supplies, airplanes and a decided edge.

His thoughts returned to the communications outpost Eldridge and his people had turned up in Northern Kuwait. He had no doubt the outpost carried considerable weight pinpointing today's attack. Talia Alireza and her people were standing by, ready to take the fight back to Iraq as soon as things cleared here. The Executioner figured that even as quick as they'd be able to make the insertion, they'd still be miles off the lead regarding effective retaliation.

Khalid Shawiyya had entrenched himself too deeply to be removed easily. It was shaping up to be a very hard, very nasty war.

There was no warning of the incoming Tomahawks. Suddenly they were just there, wreaking havoc among the stalled tanks. Carrying thousand-pound conventional warheads, the missiles ate through the Iraqi armored cavalry like acid. Panicked by the destruction raining down around them, other tank commanders fell prey to the remaining tankbusters scattered across the desert floor.

Within seconds it was over. Multicolored smoke whirled from gutted tanks and smoking pits blasted in the expanse of sand. Bodies, some burned beyond recognition, some still on fire, and others seemingly untouched, lay draped across the war machines and the ground. At least forty more staggered or ran away from the vicinity. Iraqi jets and the occasional allied fighter continued to litter the landscape.

"Scarlet Leader One," a new voice broke in over the com/net, "be advised that Chickenhawk Unit has arrived. Over."

Bolan glanced up from the HueyCobra's weapon control systems and saw the formation of F-14 Tomcats winging in from the eastern coastline when Grimaldi pointed them out. "Welcome aboard, Chickenhawk Unit. Your tactical movement will be plotted through Azure Typhoon Leader. Scarlet Leader One out."

Obvious confusion passed through the aerial Iraqi troops. The jets sought higher ground, more room. Allied forces closed in without hesitation, catching the planes between a classic pincer movement.

"Home Plate," Bolan called out, "this is Scarlet Leader One. Get Fast Strike moving and out of the gate. Out." He raked 20 mm cannon fire across an Iraqi jet, pushing the limits of his weapon, scored on the fuselage and caused it to pull out of the attack flight path it had been in. Rolling over, the jet was exposed to one of the Tomcats, which hit it with a Phoenix air-to-air missile, then flew through the resulting debris.

Below, the sandbag barriers surrounding Kuwait City were briefly opened to release twenty TOW-armed war buggies. Spurts of desert sand flared out behind the fat tires when the drivers reached for speed. They encountered no enemy fire when they approached the mired tank command. Fast Strike constituted eighty percent of the available war buggies. The allied heavy armor stayed behind in case any unpleasant surprises popped up.

Working the target areas Grimaldi presented to him, the Executioner became a part of the weapons systems, firing as much by instinct as by cybernetic input. The man was only as good as the machine, and the machine was only as good as the man. When he ran out of Hellfire missiles, he relied on the 20 mm cannon until there were no targets left.

The skies cleared. The allied forces were once more in command of everything they could see.

"Take us up, Jack." Bolan leaned back against the thin padding of his seat and eased the strain aching between his shoulders.

Grimaldi powered the rotor engines, and the desert floor beneath them dropped away. Carnage was spread over the burning sand for miles in all directions. A broken-backed Iraqi Mirage had impacted against the sandbag barrier shielding the outer perimeters of Kuwait City. Flames danced madly as crews worked to douse them. It was impossible to tell how many casualties lay below. Concerted effort would have to be applied before more than guesswork could enter the field reports. The war buggies had already secured the forward reaches of the main battle area. A foot patrol circulated within the wreckage of tanks and jet fighters, serving a number of purposes: taking prisoners, killing soldiers who continued to resist and relaying information to the medical units standing by.

Bolan monitored the communications filtering through the com/net. None of it was for him. His purpose had been served. Surprisingly, in spite of the Scud attack and the delayed warning the allied forces had received concerning the ground and air attacks, they had held the line. But the numbers didn't encourage him to think Shawiyya had expended all the forces the man had at his control. An army, well fed, well trained and well equipped had been left over after the first Iraqi conflict. There would be no turning back now, and the Executioner knew it. He also knew the Stony Man teams had never faced a more willing or more able enemy.

Over to the south he caught the first lazy wing sweeps of a vulture. In seconds three others joined the first.

Bolan pointed the carrion eaters out to Grimaldi. "A reminder, Jack, that war's just another link in nature's food chain, not the sign of a civilized mind at all."

"Yeah," Grimaldi said softly. "Problem is, Mack, we don't have the luxury of making war against civilized people."

There was harsh truth in the pilot's words, and Bolan was soldier enough to know it. "Take us in," he said, "and let's see if we can up the ante to something that gives even the barbarian in Shawiyya something to think about."

IMAGES FLICKERED across the screen of the small color monitor mounted on Barbara Price's desk. The static hum of the cybernetic circuitry around her filled her mind and tugged at her cycling thoughts. No sound filtered through the closed door connecting her office with Kurtzman's world.

Though designed to be physically removed from the outside environs if necessary, Stony Man Farm was cued into the international heartbeat through state-of-the-art hardware. Some days it felt as if she had the rest of the world as next-door neighbors. When things were going well, she enjoyed the feeling. When she had to watch as sometimes whole countries fell apart, it became frustrating because she couldn't help but ask herself if there was something she could do. It was hard to let things go when she was out of the office.

An amber light flared to life on the phone. Price took a final sip of her lukewarm coffee, stabbed the light and brought the receiver to her ear. "Hello."

"I've got the New York police commissioner on the line, Ms. Price," the Stony Man switchboard operator said.

"Thank you. I'll take it." Price leaned back in the chair and massaged the back of her neck.

The line clicked through.

"Hello, this is Commissioner Ted Gypsum." His voice sounded controlled, tight with anger.

Price swept her fingers through the commissioner's file, which was spread out on the cluttered desktop before her. Pictures, facts and personal data lay revealed at a glance. Dirt was scattered there, too. Some of it was legitimate, Price knew, and much of it was speculative. Still, she didn't relish the thought of playing hardball unless she had no choice, and she worked hard to make sure she always had a number of choices. The stills of the commissioner as a young high school sports figure and later as a running back for the Syracuse University football team caught her eye. She leaned forward again and thumbed through them, thinking she might have her hook.

She pitched her voice low, adding a touch of sultry sexuality and hints at a Southern background. It was no Scarlett O'Hara, but she thought it would cause him automatically to think a little less guardedly about the intellect on the other end of the line. "Hello, Commissioner Gypsum. My name's Grace Keller. I'm a special agent with the Federal Bureau of Investigation based here in Quantico. I'm glad you could call me back. Flying to New York City today would have wrecked my agenda."

Gypsum's voice remained rough. "Well, Special Agent Keller—"

"Please call me Grace. Special Agent Keller just sounds entirely too formal."

"Grace. I'm sorry to have to tell you that your presence here might be required, after all. I've got three of your people up here who shot the shit—pardon my French—out of one of our buildings and killed nearly two dozen people, who, I might add, haven't been proved guilty of any crimes. Now I'm not an expert on how you people normally conduct your business, but that kind of fuckup, uh, behavior isn't tolerated where I come from."

The commissioner was watching his profanity. Price silently congratulated herself. The man had unconsciously moved from the offensive to the defensive. All she had to do was tip him over the edge. "Didn't you receive the files I faxed to you, Commissioner?"

"Yes. They're here in front of me now."

"Have you had time to look through them?"

"Yes. Some. My time hasn't exactly been free."

It was hard to come out of defensive posture. Price knew from experience. "I'm sure you noted the faces and names of the known terrorists you rounded up in that group." Stony Man Farm coffers had paid an exorbitantly high price for copies of stills and video footage photographers had shot of the extraction from the building earlier that morning. The faces that had been revealed had been quickly matched up to the data base Kurtzman and his people had set up regarding known terrorist activity stemming from the Middle East and Iraq in particular.

"Granted. Some of these people appear to be the ones you people were searching for. But my question is this—why wasn't my office told about the investigation the FBI had going on in my town?"

"It was the hope of this office that we could have taken care of the problem quietly."

"Quietly? Special Agent Keller, one of your men called 911 and told the dispatcher the building was wired to explode. Need I explain to you the kind of stress that put our frontline troops through?"

"No, Commissioner, you don't. I'm quite able to see for myself where you have cause to be agitated." Price tapped the photos of the collegiate running back catching game-winning passes. "But I'm also hoping you know how to be a team player when the chips are down. If my office had contacted yours about the terrorist cell operating out of your city, chances are some of your people would have died in the encounter. True?"

"Yes, but—"

"And was anyone hurt by our operation?"

"No."

"I'd say it came off rather cleanly, wouldn't you?"

"I don't like being stonewalled out of the play, Agent Keller."

A low buzzing echoed in the background of the connection. A warning light lit up on the security panel in front of Barbara Price, letting her know the phone line was being tapped and traced. Neither would be a problem. She didn't intend to say anything that would incriminate herself or Able Team. And the trace would lead to the heart of Quantico's FBI headquarters where Kurtzman's cybernetic magic would dump it.

Price made her voice a trifle harder. "I can appreciate that, Commissioner. I know you're a heads-up type of player." She studied the photos again, thinking about repeating the subconscious appeal to his team spirit, thinking about tracking onto a threat to make him look foolish in the media if he didn't quiet down and go along. "How soon can you cut our people up there free?"

"I couldn't give you even a guess," Gypsum replied. "My people are pretty rankled by the whole situation. Once the story breaks on this, they're going to be left with egg on their faces, and they know it."

Price let a few seconds slide by to give the impression of hesitation. "How about if we struck a bargain, Commissioner?"

"What kind of bargain?" The man was instantly wary.

"If you let our people go, I'm sure I can convince my superiors that the FBI needn't try for any of the ink that comes in off this investigation. As far as the media is concerned, they can be told that New York's Finest handled the whole operation from beginning to end."

Gypsum remained silent.

"Well, Commissioner?"

"Do you know how much trouble we've had confirming your people were associated with the FBI?"

"They were on special assignment. It's not unusual for everyone in the home office not to know what every field agent's doing at one given time."

"I understand. I just want to make sure it stays that way. I don't want any reporters suddenly turning up a link to the FBI that yanks the rug out from under our feet up here."

"Rest assured," Price said, "that's the furthest thing from my mind." And it was. Like the other Stony Man teams, Able was supposed to be keeping as low a profile as possible. Even though sanctioned by the President, their presence could be hard to explain. "Do we have a deal?"

"With the assurance that you'll get your people out of my town within the hour?"

"There's a mountain of information to sort through there," Price objected. She didn't let the elation she felt color her voice.

"You have my promise that as soon as we find something the FBI can use, we'll forward it."

"It appears, Commissioner, that you have me over a barrel." Actually the computer equipment the NYPD had confiscated from the terrorist hardsite had already been rendered unusable by Kurtzman.

"Yes, Grace, I do." Gypsum chuckled in satisfaction. "And I want you to know I have every intention of keeping you there. This whole conversation has been taped. If you try to double-cross me, I'll start blasting you and your people in the media. Something along the lines of how the days of the FBI deciding what's best for the general public were thought to have died with J. Edgar Hoover. I know some reporters who'd have a field day playing up the danger-to-the-community-at-large angle this story could be painted with."

"I'm sure you do, Commissioner." Price added an underlying chill to her voice, but knew she had the man in the mind-set she needed him to be. Gypsum wouldn't want to rock the deal he'd set up for himself, so his inquiries to the FBI would die off, leaving less loose ends for the Stony Man infrasecurity people to worry about. "I'm to assume our agents will be released soon?"

"Within the hour. And keep in mind the tape of this conversation."

"Commissioner Gypsum," Price said with downright insulted frost, "might I remind you that where I come from a person's word is his or her bond."

"Yes, ma'am, and in New York we make our own insurance. You have a good day, Grace."

"And you." Price cradled the receiver and permitted herself a smile. The deal would work out all the way around, and it would put Able Team back on the streets, operating on the information they'd culled from the terrorist cell.

She stood and stretched. On her way to the coffeemaker she studied the map of the Middle East. Her thoughts turned to Bolan, and she wondered how good a choice Talia Alireza had been to aid the man in his covert missions on the other side of the Iraqi border. She sighed as she poured a fresh cup of coffee. There was simply no way of telling until the final few hands were played out.

She had to admit that it was more than just a little professional pride that kept her from thinking the intelligence leak might be coming from Stony Man systems themselves. Yet the only other source would have to be Alireza. In a way it was catch-22. If the leak hadn't come from one of her spheres of influence, it had certainly come from another. She didn't know which she would rather have herself question—her judgment of people or her supervision of Stony Man security systems.

The phone rang again. This time it was the direct access line she had to Hal Brognola in the White House.

The big Fed spoke without preamble. "Barb, I wanted you to know the news as soon as it had been confirmed. The allied forces are about to recommence the bombing of Baghdad from the Saudi theater."

Price looked at the wall clock. "How soon?"

"They're outfitting now. The Joint Chiefs of Staff issued the order on the spot."

"Striker and Valkyrie are on their way behind the lines."

"I know. See if you can reach him and pull him back until some of this mess has been straightened out. Since the Scud attacks on Kuwait, Saudi Arabia and Israel this morning, the allied generals feel they have no recourse but some kind of instant retaliation.''

''Damn it.''

''The President feels the same way we do,'' Brognola went on. ''He knows we've got people over there, but he can't own up to it yet until the assassination of Hamoud Jaluwi has been ironed out. If he admits we've fielded teams of counterterrorist specialists over there, Jaluwi's death may come to a final resting place in our backyard and pull the whole Stony Man operation down the tube with it.''

''I know. Let me get off here and see if I can reach Striker in time to scrub the infiltration.''

Brognola cleared the line.

Price left her office and made straight for Aaron Kurtzman, who was sitting at his horseshoe-shaped desk. All secondary communications to the Stony Man teams had to go through the networks he'd established.

Kurtzman's fingers flew over the keyboard in front of him. Images on the monitor directly in front of him moved, took on new perspectives and changed colors like a chameleon.

She called his name.

He answered without breaking contact with the keyboard. ''I was just going to call you, Barb. Our intelligence-communications network *has* been breached.''

White-on-black schematics materialized on the monitor screen, growing larger as the program blew up the components. Amber lines streaked in from four sides to lock in on the target.

Stifling the urge to ask the source of the tapped intel lines, Price said, ''I need a hard line to Striker. Allied forces are readying a bombing run into Iraq. He and Alireza's team might get caught in the middle of it.''

Kurtzman turned away from the running program and looked at her, his fingers poised over the keyboard. Without warning the computer monitor in front of Kurtzman and the three wall screens extending around the room blacked out and went dead.

"Son of a bitch," Kurtzman said in a stunned voice. "They had a virus in the program. They nuked the systems." His fingers launched a new attack on the keyboards, and he bellowed out orders to the cybernetics team.

Stepping around the big man, Price lifted the telephone receiver near one of the modem pods. When she held it to her ear, only empty white sound reached her.

STANDING IN THE Oval Office awaiting the President's return, Hal Brognola glanced at his watch. If Barbara Price had been able to reach Striker, she'd have called to let him know. He kept his hand away from the phone with effort. Instead, he seized the remote control for the television across the room and thumbed up the volume.

The set was tuned to CNN; it had been since the outbreak of the threatening reengagement in the Middle East. Brognola had been watching the station so long he recognized all of the reporters without the footnote announcements near the bottom of the screen. The Kuwait-based news team was glossing over the highlights at the city's defensive measures against the latest Iraqi attack, saying that the effort was supervised by Colonel Rance Pollock. He added that more information on the elusive colonel would be broadcast as it became available.

Brognola made a mental note of the reporters' curiosity regarding the erstwhile colonel. It was possible, if they weren't careful, that news agents could do what no hostile gun had been able to so far—take out the Executioner and render the man and his talents virtually unusable in the coming conflict.

The President entered the office, flanked by two young Secret Service men.

"Give us some air, gentlemen," the President said without turning to face his escort.

"Yes, sir, Mr. President." They went out of the room as silently as shadows.

"Anything, Hal?" The President gestured toward the television.

"Nothing new, sir." Brognola turned the sound down a little. "We might be too late to halt Striker and his team's infiltration into Iraq. We've had some problems with our communications relays."

The President hesitated for a moment. "I don't want to lose the man at this point in the game."

"Neither do I. There's no possibility of delaying the bomb runs?" Brognola asked.

"Not without attracting direct inquiries from every top military brass and head of state in the allied forces. There's no reason to wait that they're aware of."

Brognola sighed quietly. "Yeah, I know. Any hesitation on our part is just going to make Shawiyya and his terrorist cohorts wonder just what the hell's going on. That kind of thinking could ultimately be just as deadly to Striker and his covert team."

The President sat at his desk. "You're sure Striker will still attempt this foray into Iraq after the attack on Kuwait? I understand we took some pretty heavy casualties during that engagement."

"We did. And, yeah, he will. His target's a communications base Desert Lightning pinpointed that's believed to be used to target sites in Kuwait and possibly Israel. His line of reasoning is that the sooner he knocks that outpost out, the more lives he can save."

"A very dedicated man, our Striker."

"Yes, sir."

"Chances are, Hal, that even if he knew about the aerial assault we've got in the works, he'd still take his chances with the communications base."

"I keep telling myself that, and I know it's true. But I just wish he knew for certain how deep he was going to be in it in the next little while."

Abruptly the scene on the television monitor changed, filled with the words Special Bulletin, then focused on the anchor based in the CNN home studio. "This just in from Baghdad," the newsman said. "It appears that President Khalid Shawiyya was assassinated sometime this morning. Representatives of the Iraqi government are citing American Special Forces as responsible."

Brognola turned up the audio without being asked.

"Although these statements have been issued without support," the anchorman continued, "Shawiyya's government says they will have all the proof the world will need within the next few days."

On screen the anchor melted away as a page from another video dropped unscrolled. "We're taking you now to Baghdad as our reporters there bring you the latest word on this fast-breaking story."

5

"It's a very fine funeral procession," Semyon Zagladin said. "Shawiyya would be very proud."

Hamoud Jaluwi turned to look at the resident agent the KGB had inserted into Baghdad. "Khalid Shawiyya was an idiot, a cur. His body should have been burned and his name offered to history with no respect at all." He shifted his attention to the long stream of people winding through the streets of Baghdad four stories below. At the forefront was Khalid Shawiyya's ornate coffin, carried by officers of his Republican guard that had ultimately betrayed him at Jaluwi's command. "Instead your machinations have turned him into a martyr."

"Your movement, and ours, needed a martyr at this moment," Zagladin said. The Russian agent was big but maintained a dapper appearance despite his size and the cheap clothing he wore. His hands were thick and broad, reflective of the man's physical appearance and the expansiveness of his moods.

Jaluwi leaned on the windowsill and peered down. Military jeeps with flashing sirens trundled slowly ahead and behind the coffin. A wall of Republican guards kept the crowd back. People cried out so loudly that they could be heard inside the hotel room where Jaluwi stood. Parents held their children on their shoulders so that they could see the passage of the body. Foreign reporters were allowed through the lines, one at a time in the presence of the guardsmen, to take pictures and videos of the dead Iraqi president. The coffin had been left open. Shawiyya rested inside, hands folded across his chest, dressed in full military uniform with the evening sun glinting off the dozens of medals across his broad chest. Flowers from baskets carried by veiled young woman were strewn across the streets in front of the procession. Four military helicopters, armed with sharpshooters and rocket launchers, hovered expectantly over the streets like birds of prey.

"If you don't mind my saying so, Comrade Jaluwi," Zagladin stated, "you sound as if you're experiencing pangs of jealousy over your comrade's fate. Your own demise wasn't nearly as ornate or histrionic."

Jaluwi reflected on the faked funeral that had buried his name and given him his present invisibility to the enemies of the united Middle Eastern factions. His fingers brushed the healing wound inscribed on his forehead. There was a hint of truth to the Russian's words. "You have the wrong perception."

"Do I? If so, I stand corrected."

Biting down on the rush of anger that threatened to consume him, Jaluwi picked up the field glasses from the coffee table beside the window. The room was well furnished, with American pieces instead of the traditional Middle Eastern decor. Although he'd noticed Zagladin's more obvious ease with American things than with those that were Arab, he didn't note it aloud. As chief KGB liaison in Iraq, Zagladin was a man who commanded power, one Jaluwi didn't intend to offend as yet.

He focused the binoculars on the open casket. All too aware of the Soviet Union's interest in the Middle East, Jaluwi was equally aware that the terrorist strikes and international war effort would have come to naught without Russian support.

Centering on Khalid Shawiyya's face, Jaluwi increased the magnifications of the binoculars until he could see the raw wound crumpling in the dead man's forehead just slightly left of center. Burned black around the edges from the proximity of the gunshot, the bullet hole went in small and led to the empty cavity where the back of Shawiyya's head had been. The folds of the sapphire-blue silk pillow obscured the yawning exit wound.

When he executed Shawiyya, Jaluwi hadn't been thinking of the task he was laying before the morticians.

"However," Zagladin went on, "we agree with your assessment of Shawiyya. That is, of course, the reason we chose instead to go along with you."

"Your political leaders went along with me," Jaluwi said, "because I was most in a position to give them what they want. Without me Russia would have no chance at all at recouping some of its former glories in the international arena. And that is to say nothing of the Soviet wish for warm-water ports and a sustained sphere of influence in the Middle East." He laid the binoculars down and watched as the funeral procession continued on through the street.

In the distance the new Iraqi flag, designed by the late president, flew at half-mast.

"We need each other for now," Jaluwi went on. "For the time that means we can't be enemies and hope to achieve our goals. I don't pander to my ego and tell myself the KGB chose to work through me because my politics are right."

"You're a wise man, Comrade."

"Am I? Sometimes I wonder, friend Zagladin. My own following in Syria was growing once more, strengthened by the chest beating the Americans were doing in their own country. President Hafez Assad's control over my country is weakening. Perhaps, had I been a little more patient, I'd have found myself as a head of state in due time, anyway."

Shrugging, Zagladin crossed the living room of the small apartment and took a chocolate chip cookie from a bag on the coffee table. He sniffed it expectantly, then took a small bite.

Jaluwi had taken note of the Russian's preference for American sweets, as well. His personal aide was under standing orders to see to it that Zagladin's appetites were catered to without fail.

"We have more to offer you than that," Zagladin said, "and you know it. With us Syria won't be your only prize. You could well end up as political spokesman for most of the Middle East as it is now known. When you start having your doubts about the things we've put into motion, just repeat the name of it to yourself. United Arab Republic. And whatever you decide to call the office overseeing the UAR, *you* will be its leader."

Returning the Soviet agent's gaze full measure, Jaluwi said nothing. The KGB had known of his political aspirations long before he'd known of their willingness to help him realize them. But everything had its price. It remained to be seen whose ambitions proved more costly—his own, or the KGB's.

"WHAT DO YOU THINK of this big American?" Jimoh asked.

There was only a brief hesitation in Talia Alireza's hands as she resecured her hair with the leather thong around her head. Her unit had kept to themselves while the Iraqi attack had blunted itself against the combined might of the allied troops. A few roving bands of terrorists had penetrated the city's defenses and had been intent on dividing the attention of the allied defenders. Alireza and her group had accounted for three such bands while the final trumps were being played west of the city.

Finished with her hair, Alireza picked up the Galil Model 223 ARM combat rifle and scanned the broken rind of Kuwait City through the dust-covered windshield of the truck they'd confiscated for their use. "Striker seems to be a very capable man."

Jimoh scowled. Big, black and burly, with a gleaming shaven head, her second resembled some mythical hero carved from barbaric legend. "He's a man who follows his heart, Talia. Such men are dangerous. They can incite otherwise intelligent people to break their backs struggling against an insurmountable obstacle."

The woman flashed him a mirthless smile. "And you see Iraq as an insurmountable obstacle?"

"I didn't say that."

She looked away and stared at the clouds of black smoke stemming from the fires started by the Scud missiles. "The American and allied forces have beaten Iraq once before."

"Things are different now," Jimoh argued. "The Americans and their allies think they're ready for another war, but this won't be the same as last time. Never before was the anti-Western sentiment spread so widely. Never before did the Iraqi conflict erupt within the United States as it now has."

"You think they'll break?"

Jimoh shrugged. "I don't know. Their concept of war is much different than ours. Of them all, only the British truly understand what winning is all about. The Americans think that if their enemy has surrendered, the war is over and they've won. The British would go in, set fire to the homes of their enemy and carefully observe them as they sought to rebuild. That wasn't done with Saddam Hussein or Khalid Shawiyya. The Russian soldiers we've encountered are enough to let us know that things aren't completely as we believe them to be."

Turning to face her second, Alireza kept her features neutral but knew she couldn't conceal the fire in her eyes. "What would you have us do?"

Jimoh sighed. "It isn't about what I would have us do, Talia. Personally I'd like to take a stand against the Iraqis and their terrorist allies. We've fought men like them over much of the globe, you and I, and we know them for the vermin they can be. Professionally I'd be willing to give the Americans back their money and sit this one out. No matter how it goes these times are going to be very costly to fighting men. We don't fight grudge matches. We fight winnable battles, undertake attainable goals. That's one of the reasons we've never worked the Middle East. And you yourself set down that edict."

"We sat out the last one," Alireza said in a small voice.

"And we could just as easily sit out this one." Jimoh shifted, turning more toward her. His big hands were knotted around the steering wheel.

Alireza said nothing.

"You have ties to these lands," Jimoh said. "There's no getting around that. And as much as you have tried to deny it, there are feelings within you concerning the fate of these countries. You have family in Iraq. Your past is there."

"The only thing in Iraq," the woman replied, "is a little girl's foolish dreams of a home that never was. You can't keep lies with you forever. We both know that."

Jimoh nodded. "So you understand why it is that I have to ask you, my lady, whether it's your head or your heart that you follow now."

Tightening her grip on her rifle, Alireza shook her head. "I can't truthfully answer, Jimoh. Not even to myself. There was so much confusion in me after the first American war with Iraq."

"Just remember, you have thirty men following you. So far we have only had three wounded. None have died. If you find you're following your heart as Striker is, listen to it, but think with your head.''

She smiled and placed a hand on the big man's arm. "You're a true friend, Jimoh. I expect you to help me keep it all straight."

A burst of static rattled the radio mounted under the dash. Her unit's electronics people had installed it as soon as they'd confiscated the vehicle and gotten it running again. "Valkyrie, this is Striker. Over."

She picked up the receiver and thumbed the transmit button. "Striker, you have Valkyrie. Over."

"How's your group? Over."

"Intact. Three wounded, but only one of them won't be able to make the hop with us. Over."

"Do you need medical assistance for your wounded? Over."

"Negative, Striker. We've managed to sort things out for ourselves. Our wounded has found a safe place to hole up until we're able to return for him. Over."

"Understood. Are you people ready to move out? Over."

"We've been waiting for your call, Striker. Over."

Lightness touched the big man's grim voice. "Acknowledged, Valkyrie. Our timetable has been slightly skewed, but we're in the green again." He gave her the coordinates for the rendezvous.

Taking her map case from her trousers, she found the site quickly.

"Be there in fifteen," Striker said. "It's jump straight into hell after that. And from my estimate we'll be getting there after dark. Over."

Alireza checked her watch. "My estimate agrees with yours. Don't keep us waiting. Valkyrie out."

Striker cleared.

Jimoh keyed the ignition. The truck started noisily as the big engine vibrated to life. Without a word the big man reached into a pocket of his Camou jacket and took out a crumpled pack of cigarettes. He shook one up and offered it.

The woman looked at it. "I quit."

"I know. That's how I knew you didn't have any." His laughter filled the interior of the truck and took some of her uncertainty away.

She accepted the cigarette, ignited it with the lighter she carried for various intents and purposes and breathed in the smoke.

Jimoh drove with confidence despite the sorry condition of the bombed streets. He never once glanced at her map case lying open on the seat between them.

At times she envied him his sense of direction. No matter what had faced them in the past, Jimoh had always taken his time and let the destination ultimately draw him in rather than forcing himself or his unit through the defensive perimeters. Alireza had always felt the need to crash through barriers, to take the ground or terminate the targets she'd been hired to take or terminate. With Jimoh in charge the mercenary unit would have worked less often because the big man wasn't as driven as she was. With her in charge, without Jimoh to goad her into thinking about days instead of hours, the unit would have worked more dangerously. Together they made a good team.

Tired, she closed her eyes. Without warning the image of a little girl staring into the muddy water of the Tigris River looked back at her. For a moment she could smell the city behind her. Baghdad in her memory was a place marked indelibly by the river where her family had lived—the smell of the water, the fish, the taste of fruits that could be wheedled from the hawkers in the marketplace, the sun-blasted mud bricks that formed most of the houses, dominated by the golden-domed mosques.

For a moment she saw her mother there, thought of the woman as she rarely let herself do, then banished the memories before they could hurt her further.

"THERE," Jack Grimaldi said. The pilot cut the jeep through the fresh debris strewn across the street and headed for the contingent of Desert Lightning troops carrying wounded into the makeshift hospital. The building had once housed a wealthy bank with huge interests sunk into the Kuwaiti oil field. Those days were gone, along with the profits and the upper third of the seven-story building. Enough remained of the lower two floors to house the wounded and a medical staff equipped well enough to stabilize most of the worst trauma cases before flying them out.

Mack Bolan yanked the radio free of the patch job he'd done after disembarking from the Huey and flipped the power source switch back to DC. He shoved it into his shoulder pack, slid into it, then hooked the transmit and reception wires back into his ear-throat headset. The radio would beep if Talia Alireza or her group tried to contact him, leaving him free to monitor the other channels used by the Desert Lightning group and the allied troops.

Colonel Eldridge stepped through the open ranks of his men as Grimaldi brought the jeep to a skidding halt in front of the medical center. He saluted Bolan stiffly, eyes forward like a man at attention. "Ten-*hut*," he barked to his men.

Desert Lightning snapped to attention despite their disheveled appearance. Other men in the American contingent of the allied forces snapped to, as well.

"At ease, Colonel," Bolan said. He fired off a return salute, then stepped out of the jeep holding his steel helmet by the chin straps. "As you were, gentlemen," he said to the rest of the enlisted men. "We're standing down for the time being. Smoke 'em if you got 'em."

"Not anywhere around my OR or you'll pay hell," an American officer in surgical garb warned. He looked at Bolan sheepishly. "Sir."

The Executioner let a worn smile crease his face. "Duly noted and amended, Captain Trainor."

The captain saluted, then grabbed the end of a litter and guided it inside the building.

"Eldridge," Bolan said as he stepped into the dank shadows of the building, "you're with me."

"Yes, sir." Eldridge followed.

Grimaldi brought up the rear.

Bolan scanned the interior of the hospital. Wrecking crews were still at work altering the floor space to make more room for medical equipment. Translucent plastic sheet strips ran from ceiling to floor to separate areas already cleaned up and being used as operating theaters. The sound of hammers and crowbars mixed with the noises made by medical saws and drills and heart-lung machines. Blood covered the broken tile floor in a number of places. Sawdust, created by whining gas-powered chain saws used to remove built-in furniture and cabinets, was recycled and used to soak up spilled body fluids from the floor. Teams worked through the dozen or more ORs, spreading sawdust down after each patient was removed, then sweeping it away so that the next operation could begin less than a minute later. Voices, some tinged with hysteria, others on the edge of panic, and more speaking various degrees of calm created an audible undercurrent in the cavernous space created in the first floor.

"In here," Bolan said, indicating one of the small offices in the southwest corner of the ground floor.

They threaded through the gurneys of wounded and dead. Litter bearers worked nonstop, taking some, depositing others. Men who paused to rest were immediately hooked up to blood transfusion units. Even those who weren't wounded were being bled.

In the office Bolan put his helmet on a desk covered by fallen ceiling tiles. Grimaldi pulled the door closed behind them and stood guard beside it. With a wave of his arm the Executioner cleared glass-encased documents and awards from the paneled walls. Glass shattered as they hit the floor. He cleared a work area with a booted foot.

Withdrawing a topographical map from his shoulder pack, Bolan spread it against the blank expanse of wall and used surgical tape from an ammo pouch to hold it in place. "Colonel."

"Yes, sir," Eldridge responded.

The map encompassed all of Kuwait and the eastern borders of Iraq.

"It's twenty-five miles to Al-Jahrah," Bolan said. His finger touched the city east of Kuwait Bay. "If the Desert Lightning Unit moves from Kuwait City by 2300 hours tonight, can they be in place and entrenched by 0500 hours tomorrow morning?"

"Full cav and armored, sir?" Eldridge asked.

"Yes."

"It'll be pressing the envelope you've chosen, but it can be done."

"Good enough. See that it is."

"Begging the colonel's pardon," Eldridge said, "but aren't you forgetting the terrorist communications outpost we informed you of near Multa?"

"No. Rest assured, that base will be history before Desert Lightning moves into the area."

If Eldridge had any doubts, he didn't voice them.

Bolan took the map down and folded it. "I'm going to be away for a time. You have full command over Desert Lightning until my return. Your orders once you reach your destination are to stand down, make yourselves as inconspicuous as possible and be prepared to take down another ground assault against this city.''

''A holding action, sir?''

''For now.''

Eldridge's cheeks reddened. ''Sir, I was told from the beginning that the Desert Lightning command was to be an offensive unit. My men and I have geared ourselves to strike out at those Iraqi bastards, not sit on the sidelines and play clay pigeon.''

Bolan met the man's gaze. ''We'll be striking out at them, soldier, but we're going to do it on our terms. Not theirs.''

''They'll be weak after that assault we just busted up,'' Eldridge said. ''Now could be the time to press the advantage.''

''Now isn't the time. During this last attack it has also been discovered that Russian agents, operating within the terrorist and Iraqi periphery, were deep in Kuwait City with top-secret information concerning American activity here. Communications between allied forces and the Joint Chiefs of Staff have been breached. The attack on Kuwait City and this defensive post could be another feint designed to draw our strength out into the open where it can be destroyed. For the moment, until more deployment schematics can be worked out and put into play, and the Russian interests can be quantified, Desert Lightning and the Navy are the only things keeping this city free. Without our position here allied troops will be limited in their ground attack. If we can hold on to it, chances are we'll be able to cut deeply into Iraqi territory when the time comes. You'll get all the offensive you'll want then.''

''Yes, sir.'' Eldridge didn't sound convinced.

''Do you understand your orders?'' Bolan asked.

''Yes, sir.''

''Then carry them out.''

Eldridge saluted smartly, performed an about-face and headed for the door.

Grimaldi opened it and saluted.

"And, Colonel," Bolan said.

Eldridge turned. "Sir?"

"Good luck."

"Yes, sir."

Grimaldi closed the door behind the man. "Aggressive son of a bitch, isn't he?"

Bolan put the map back in his shoulder pack. "Any officer worth his salt is. Give him a little more time, some seasoning, Eldridge could make a hell of a warrior. Things coming at him like this, though, it's going to make or break him damn quick."

"Guy had an impressive record during the Grenada invasion and the first Iraqi conflict," Grimaldi said. "Looking at him, I'd say he's wanting a larger share of the glory this time around."

"You might be misreading him. Eldridge is driven, yeah, but I haven't been able to put my finger on what pushes him right now." He checked his watch. "You've got seven minutes to get us to the airstrip."

"Piece of cake," Grimaldi replied.

Once outside, Grimaldi climbed behind the wheel of the jeep and keyed the engine to life. He let out the clutch the same time as he hit the horn to clear the way.

Bolan studied the destruction of the city around him. It was hard to tell where the old wounds left off and the new ones began, except when the bodies were still lying in the wreckage. A Marine unit was already using confiscated civilian backhoes and bulldozers to dig community graves. Others, aided by the citizens of Kuwait, dragged corpses toward the openings in the hard-baked earth.

The city was a study in death.

"Once you make the jump," Grimaldi said as he pulled on the wheel and aimed them down a side street, "there ain't going to be a damn thing I can do for you."

"I know," Bolan said. He checked his gear mechanically and pulled the parachute pack from the rear of the jeep.

"Still wish we'd gotten to know Alireza and her people better," the pilot said. "Barb might have a lot of trust in her. Me, I keep reservations till I see somebody sky."

Bolan gave his friend a crooked grin. "If something goes wrong, Jack, you can always tell her I told you so."

"Terrific."

Less than a minute later the airstrip came into view. The Lockheed C-130 Hercules looked ominous sitting at the other end of the runway. The big plane was painted night-black and was outfitted with 25 mm and 40 mm automatic cannon as well as a 105 mm howitzer. The infiltration was supposed to be done quietly, but Bolan knew the covert team wasn't going gently into that good night.

The Executioner found Talia Alireza and her shock troops waiting when Grimaldi pulled the jeep to a halt. Within seconds they were airborne, flying into the approaching cover of night.

"SOMEBODY SLIPPED a goddamn virus into our system," Kurtzman explained.

Barbara Price had a hard time understanding him because he held a small flashlight between his teeth.

The darkness sweltering through the cybernetics command post at Stony Many Farm had a fetid breath. When the enemy program had crashed the computer systems, it had also shut down all power to the complex. Without the air-conditioning the room had heated up quickly.

"Take this," Kurtzman said, jiggling the flashlight between his teeth.

Price took the light and kept it aimed at the wall circuitry board where his hands were busy splicing electrical wires. Dead fuses littered the carpeted ground under the wheels of his chair.

A spark jumped, flamed blue and white in the dark. Kurtzman muttered an obscenity and yanked his hand back. "Well, that's a good sign. Means we still have power from the main lines."

Price curbed the impatience shooting through her. Thirty-seven minutes had elapsed since the shutdown of the Stony Man systems. In that time all hell could have broken loose in the Middle Eastern theater where Phoenix Force, Striker and Grimaldi were. Her stomach knotted as her imagination summoned up another wave of worst-case scenarios.

Moving carefully, Kurtzman spliced more wires and wrapped black electrical tape around their exposed lengths.

Behind them, down in the pit where the other computer hardware was used, a small corps of technicians brought in new computers, disk drives, monitors and printers. As fast as an old unit could be taken out, a new unit was installed. Whining noise from a handful of battery-powered drills filled the cavern of the computer room.

"How did the Russians plant the virus?" Price asked.

"I regularly scan the files that I can get into," Kurtzman answered. "During the past few months somebody slipped it into an area where they could be sure I'd penetrate. A file that can't be easily broken. If it could be broken at all. The designer could have programmed a systems coma worm that would activate as soon as it was searched for and discovered. Hell, I knew that going in, but I couldn't just back away and hope for the best. We needed to know."

"I agree."

"Problem is, we've lost a hell of a lot of time."

"It means the KGB knows about us."

"They've known about us for a long time, Barb. Since before the Farnsworth fiasco when April Rose and Konzaki were killed." The big man's hand trembled as he wrapped tape.

It was also during that time, Price remembered, that Kurtzman had received the bullet that had severed his spinal cord.

"The beautiful thing about computers," Kurtzman said, "is that you can use one to go anywhere, penetrate all kinds of cybernetic defenses. The downside is that you, in turn, can be penetrated, as well. I'm just surprised it hasn't happened before."

"What about the phone lines, electricity and everything else?"

Kurtzman flashed a mirthless grin. "My doing," he said. "When you know you're about to have your electronic brains blown out, what's your best defense?"

Price didn't know. She was a computer systems user, not a designer. She shook her head.

"You blow them out yourself."

"You're responsible for this?"

"Yep. I designed another worm, placed it into the system myself a few years back and updated it with every breakthrough I learned about or figured out. It's only purpose was to shut our systems down before the alien program could zap us first."

"So your counterprogram pulled the plug on us."

"Yeah." Kurtzman tapped the circuit board cover back into place and held it there by two loose screws. "See, I know how to fix what I did. If their program had had a chance to run its course, our systems could be locked up in stasis for hours or days." He yelled a warning and the technicians ceased work. A few flicks of a series of breaker switches and the computer room hummed back to life.

Lights flashed on at once. "My destructiveness I knew I could fix in a matter of minutes."

Price crossed the room to the phone and picked it up. There was a dial tone. Some of the acid in her stomach went away.

The computer technicians went back to work laying in the new hardware.

Studying the monitor in front of his keyboard, Kurtzman hit the keys rapidly, bringing the new system on-line. "We pulled out the other hardware because it may be tainted with the KGB program. We start over fresh like this, so I don't have to worry about it coming back to haunt us. But it'll be a while before we can transcribe the intel we've gathered regarding the mission and feed it back into our system."

"Could it have been from the data Able transmitted to us?" Price asked. She punched in a number and listened to the satisfying clicks the exchanges made as they routed the call to Kuwait City.

"That's good thinking, Barb," Kurtzman said.

The wall screens flared to life around the room, filling immediately with television transmissions from around the world.

"But," Kurtzman went on, "I verified Able's discovery myself. Those programs were simple search-and-find cataloging stuff. If anything exotic had been slipped in there, I'd have known it at once."

At the other end of the phone connection the scrambler kicked into operation. A harsh screech let Price know the recording machine was ready to take her message. She put the receiver down and stared at the CNN broadcast coming from Saudi Arabia. Details of the last attack against the allied air base were being rehashed again. If Striker had been anywhere within range of the scrambler phone, the message would have been relayed to him via the special radio he carried to run the Valkyrie operation. The call had been wasted effort. Striker was already en route to Baghdad.

And there wasn't a damn thing she could do to stop him.

Her helplessness uncoiled a hard knot at the back of her skull that threatened to give birth to a blinding headache. The phone rang, distracting her, then she noticed it was on her private line. She punched the extension button and took the call at Kurtzman's desk.

"It's me," Brognola said. "Where the hell have you people been? I've been trying to call for fifteen minutes."

"Our computers were blitzed," Price replied, then gave the head Fed a brief summary of the past forty minutes.

"Striker?"

"Has already left Kuwait for the covert action we set up with Valkyrie."

"Damn it."

"My sentiments exactly, but they don't get us anywhere."

"Shift gears," Brognola suggested. "For now Striker's on his own. Much as we don't like the idea, that's how it is."

"Agreed."

"What's the skinny on Able?"

"They're on the move for the terrorist cell in Washington, D.C. With all the campaign tours being given by presidential candidates, Able is hoping to put down a potential bloodbath before it has the chance to erupt. National television has a lot of debates scheduled with prominent hopefuls around the capital. It would be quite a coup if the terrorists put some of them down while the rest of the United States looks on."

"The situation with Phoenix?"

"Unresolved."

"There's been no contact with them since the bombing of Israel?"

"No. If they weren't taken out by one of the Scuds, their silence means they're dealing with problems of their own."

"Shit. This seems more and more like a nightmare every time I look at it."

"I know, Hal." Price scanned the news on the wall screens.

"Who deep-sixed Stony Man's computers?"

"Aaron believes it was the Russians."

"It fits."

"Too well."

"Especially in light of the Russian involvement Valkyrie and Striker uncovered, and the fact that Khalid Shawiyya turned up dead. I know *we* didn't get to him, so it had to have been the Russians. Israel would have been taking credit for it already."

"Shawiyya's dead?" Price watched the news. CNN broke for another special report. Footage of the funeral procession in Baghdad streamed by in jumping clips of action and color.

"Shawiyya was assassinated sometime this morning," Brognola said. "His successor is shoving responsibility for the act toward the United States."

"Has the State Department been in contact with the Soviets?"

"If you can call it that. The State Department and the President are getting stonewalled. According to the Russians, Iraq was really our problem last time, not theirs, and they intend to expend no more manpower or materials to preserve the status quo."

"Have they been informed about the presence of Russian agents in Kuwait?"

"No. For the moment the Man has decided to hold that as his trump card. So far we have a handful of possible KGB agents who could have been operating independently. Until we get something more solid, the President is reluctant to make things any more confused or bitter than they already are.''

Price silently agreed with the President's assessment of the situation. Her mind seized on the opportunity of unleashing more of Stony Man Farm's satellite power and starting a whole new tactical investigation regarding Russian involvement with the new Gulf crisis. It could provide the allies with a whole new means of leverage.

A voice called for Kurtzman's attention. Price automatically tracked the voice, too.

At her post Carmen Delahunt had frozen a picture of the funeral procession on her monitor. She touched the keyboard, blanked the wall screen above her, then brought up the picture captured on her monitor.

It was shot from street level, blurred slightly as it swept across the sky at the military helicopters. A motel, scarred from past bombing attacks, stood prominently in the background.

"I was sweeping the faces of terrorists," Delahunt said, "using the terrorist-discriminatory programming we'd previously established. I came up with this." Her hands moved surely across the keyboard.

On the wall screen the frozen picture exploded, then became larger. It zoomed in, pixels changing and adjusting to maintain clarity, on a fourth-story window. A dark-skinned man with a recent head wound stood beside a much larger man with Slavic features.

The computer program isolated the Arab, blanked the rest of the screen, then matched him up against a computer-generated file picture. A third window opened up between the first two. In the middle window the fresh scar on the Arab's forehead was erased.

A legend box opened across the bottom of the screen and words scrolled inside. IDENTIFICATION CONFIRMED. SUBJECT IS HAMOUD JALUWI. SYRIAN. SUS-

PECTED OF BEING UNDERGROUND LEADER OF TERRORIST AGGRESSION STEMMING FROM SYRIA. PRESENT STATUS AND WHEREABOUTS: UNKNOWN.

Returning her attention to the phone, Price said, "Khalid Shawiyya may be dead, but guess who's still alive."

6

Stepping into the small room formed of white sheets and clapboard walls, Lieutenant Colonel Joshua Eldridge heard the stillness of death close in around him.

Outside the sound of dozens of hurried men working in a frenzy echoed within the cracked walls of the abandoned building. Electric fan motors had been added to the general din as soon as the kerosene generators were found and restored to use. Only harsh screams of the living clinging to pain-filled life penetrated the quietness of the dying in the makeshift room.

Seven men lay on the ground in litters before Eldridge. Two were dead, their eyes frozen in stares, their chests unmoving. Another had a sucking chest wound that showed signs of medical attention yet had been abandoned as a lost cause. Three more slept or hovered in comas awaiting final release.

The seventh man opened his eyes and looked at Eldridge. Peace molded his features. He spoke softly. "Joshua."

When Eldridge looked at the man again, he recognized him as Paul. No longer dressed in robes, Paul once more wore the uniform and stripe of a Desert Lightning private. They were the same clothes Eldridge had seen the man die in two days earlier.

"Who are you?" Eldridge asked.

Paul smiled. "Who do you think I am?"

"You're a dead man."

"And you're not?"

Icy cold swirled around Eldridge, freezing him in its grasp when he wanted to run.

"We are born into this world only to die, Joshua," Paul said. "From beginning to end that seems to be our only pursuit. The one thing that matters is the journey between the two."

Eldridge couldn't speak. His jaws ached from clenching them against the cold that grew stronger inside him.

"And your journey is going to be something special," Paul said. "Just as you always dreamed it would."

"No." Eldridge's voice was a croak.

Effortlessly Paul swung himself into a sitting position on the floor. "You are His Chosen One in this time and place. There's no escaping your fate. It's by His design that you're here now, in this position of power, able to affect the lives of so many."

"You're wrong," Eldridge said. "I take orders. I don't give them."

"But men listen to you, don't they?"

Reluctantly Eldridge nodded.

"There are others out among those fighting men who are just like yourself—holy warriors. It's your destiny to seek them out and unite them under your leadership to attain His objective. You have to bring them into the Light, make them see themselves for what they really are."

Rebelling against the hypnotic effect Paul's gaze had on him, Eldridge closed his eyes and tried to force the dead man's voice from his mind. When he blinked them open, Paul was still there.

"It's never easy being one of His Chosen," Paul said quietly. "The tasks He sets before you always seem to be impossible. At first. But with His strength the impossible always becomes possible. You will learn much about yourself and Him.''

Eldridge tried to move but couldn't. The cold that filled him was merciless.

Paul stood and gestured around them with his bleeding hands. ''You're telling yourself that your senses deceive you. Your mind is even toying with the idea that maybe you've gone mad.''

''Maybe I have,'' Eldridge agreed.

''And yet,'' Paul said, ''a piece of you wants to believe so desperately.'' He crossed his hands over his chest. ''This is your mortal father's fault, Joshua. He made a mockery of his faith and yours. You joined the military to escape the way your father made you feel about your love of God. But really you were only trying to escape the doubts your father had instilled in you.''

''My father didn't believe,'' Eldridge said, remembering all those painful episodes in his past. ''My father used the church, used the belief of others against them. He stole, lied, cheated and debauched all in the name of God. How could God allow His name to be so abused?''

''How can you let your mortal father's behavior steer you away from the calling of your spiritual father?''

''I wasn't steered away.''

''Then you believe?''

''Not in this.''

''Then in what?''

Eldridge's voice was soft. ''I don't know anymore.''

''You have lost your way?''

''I'm . . . confused at times.''

''I was sent to guide you, Joshua,'' Paul said quietly. ''Being His messenger is never easy. There are many trials and tribulations ahead of you. The way will be lonely and hard. The people you'll ultimately be able to bind to you, and to His sacred mission, will be few. Perhaps, in the end, they'll betray you just as your father did. But they know only the flesh. You've been given something much more. You have seen the proof of His interest in you through me."

"What is this objective you say He has set before me?"

Paul smiled. "A prophet's task, Joshua. Where Moses brought the Ten Commandments unto God's people and guided them into the Promised Land, you shall bring His people into the Second Coming. As Daniel was cast into the lions' dens, so shall you be cast into the maws of your enemies and His in this time and place."

"The Second Coming?"

Nodding, Paul said, "And an end to the evil that lies over the world. It's time for the great struggle, time for Him to bring His children home and end their suffering on this mortal plane. He never intended for His children to be at war with one another for so long. It's madness. There is peace awaiting everyone, and you'll help Him bring it."

Eldridge felt the world whirl dizzily around him.

"These aren't new thoughts to you," Paul said, taking a step forward. "You sensed these events coming during the last war with Iraq. They've hung heavily in your mind since the outbreak of the new conflict. You know the world can't go on this way. It has no end." He held out his hand.

Eldridge took it. At once the cold left him. He felt warm, rested. The fatigue from the past hours that had piled onto him, one after the other, was gone.

"And it's up to you to end it," Paul said fiercely. "Put yourself into His service, heart and soul, and His will shall be done."

"But how?"

"You'll know when the time is right." Paul released his hand. "Farewell, Joshua, until next we meet again."

"Wait." Eldridge lunged for the falling man, wrapped one big hand around Paul's forearm, tried to catch the man and ended up being pulled down with him. He struggled onto his hands and knees, maintaining his hold on Paul's arm.

"Colonel Eldridge!"

The voice came from behind Eldridge. On his knees now, he straightened his back and peered over his shoulder. His hand was still wrapped around Paul's wrist.

Chaplain Harvey Prescott, assigned to the Desert Lightning unit, stood halfway in the room under a fold of the white sheets. Paunchy and red-faced, the man looked exhausted by the recent demands he'd undergone. His uniform was rumpled and bloodstained but correct. Plastic gloves encased his hands. He held a Bible under his left arm. His eyes behind the steel-rimmed glasses were wide with surprise.

"Is there something I can help you with, sir?" Prescott asked as he entered the room. The sheet closed behind him and muted the outer noises.

"I thought I heard this soldier call my name," Eldridge said defensively. Despite everything he'd seen and heard, he wasn't ready to persuade others to follow him yet. And he already knew men who claimed to be close to God were the hardest of all to convert.

"Are you feeling all right, Colonel?"

"Of course I am," Eldridge snapped.

"I thought maybe the excitement, perhaps the heat—"

"What the hell are you getting at, mister?" Eldridge demanded. "I told you I was just reacting to this man calling my name. How does the way I feel have anything to do with that?"

Prescott cleared his throat uncomfortably. "Because, sir, there's no way that man could have called your name. He's been dead for the past forty minutes."

"You were obviously wrong," Eldridge said.

"And," Prescott continued, "he has no face. No lips. No mouth to call you."

Memory of the cold chill that had filled him thrilled through Eldridge again despite the oily perspiration clinging to his skin and clothing. He swiveled around to look at the man whose arm he clasped so desperately.

A bloody furrow running from scalp to chin had stopped bleeding some time ago. The sinus cavities and open mouth gaped obscenely. Broken and splintered teeth framed the lower jaw. The eyes were fractured pools of jelly.

Mastering his shock and revulsion, Eldridge lifted his hand from the dead man's arm. He stood and forced his weak and trembling knees to support him. He couldn't tear his gaze away from the corpse. The uniform didn't belong to the Desert Lightning unit, after all.

"Sir?" Prescott said.

"I'm all right, Chaplain," Eldridge said with unnecessary loudness.

"Maybe I should ask one of the doctors to have a look at you—"

Eldridge turned on the man, stepped into Prescott's personal space and glared down at the Special Forces chaplain. "You've got five minutes to get yourself organized, soldier. Desert Lightning is pulling out of Kuwait City at 2300 hours. That leaves you time to get things tied up here, scrounge up what could be the last hot meal you'll see for days or weeks and get ready to move out. And you'll be cutting it close if you're on time. Understood?"

"Yes, sir." Prescott saluted reflexively.

Hesitating just a moment, wanting to ensure the chaplain didn't find the nerve later to press the issue any further, Eldridge executed an about-face and marched out of the room. The two privates he'd assigned to be his personal security picked him up at once and fell into stride with him. If they'd heard anything of what had happened within the chaplain's office, they gave no indication.

Paul's words hammered inside Eldridge's mind. Despite the glare of the setting sun outside, the chill he'd experienced persisted. Firmly seated in the passenger seat of his jeep, the words of the Twenty-third Psalm came unbidden to his lips.

No matter what Chaplain Prescott would think he'd seen, Eldridge knew what had truly happened. For the first time in years his faith had returned to him stronger than ever. Whatever His will might be, Joshua Eldridge stood ready to carry it out. His hand tightened on his pistol butt. Whatever it took.

"I'M ON HIM," Calvin James said as he lifted the door handle and popped the latch before Rafael Encizo could bring the car to a halt. The domelight bulb had been removed so that it wouldn't give their presence away when the door opened.

Ahead of them the truck carrying Gadi Maimun stopped at the corner. The man got out and hurried toward the shadows filling the alley east of Jerusalem's Via Dolorosa. James left the back seat of the Dodge Dart in a long-striding run nearly sixty yards back from his target.

Maimun disappeared into the alley.

Dressed in a hooded robe like so many Arabs around him, James knew he wouldn't attract undue attention. Even running, especially this late at night, was acceptable. The people of the Old City were long familiar with the possibility of the kiss of a thieving assassin's knife before the Israeli soldiers started policing the city with stricter intents. It wasn't wise to be caught out in the open after dark.

James's muscles came alive reluctantly. After Katz's capture, there had been hours of inactivity and restlessness. Maimun had seemed content to wait and see what happened after Nejd's death.

On the other hand, the three remaining members of Phoenix Force had scarcely been able to contain themselves despite the needs of the mission. There had been no word from McCarter, so the fates of their missing teammates were unresolved. Contact with Bolan or Stony Man Farm had been put on hold until they had no other options.

"Calvin." Gary Manning's voice whispered into James's ear.

"Go," James responded.

"Just checking, guy. This city at night gives me palpitations."

"That's what you get for watching all those Boris Karloff mummy movies as a kid. Now get out of my head and let me do my job."

"Check. Rafael and I'll be hanging ten waiting for your call."

James made the corner of the alley, paused only a moment, then followed it around. Four other people were in the narrow, twisting alley, but only one of them was coming James's way. The Phoenix Force member reached up, drew the cowl of the hood closer and walked on. The other man never looked at him.

Maimun was in the lead, now only twenty yards away. James stripped the hood away and adjusted the ear-throat headset he wore. Beneath the robe he carried a mat-black Beretta 92-F 9 mm pistol in a shoulder rig. A Randall survival knife was sheathed along his left calf. Pockets in the robe contained a garrote and a nasty assortment of incendiary surprises that Gary Manning had arranged for close-quarters fighting, if necessary. Built along the lines of British SAS flash bombs, the special grenades were designed to disorient an enemy and buy time for an escape or assault. And the black Phoenix warrior's training as a Navy SEAL had included a number of martial arts disciplines that guaranteed, even empty-handed, he was still a dangerous opponent.

Pausing at a turn in the alley, Maimun checked his back-trail. James faded into the shadows as the terrorist's head came around. His right hand was loose, ready to dive inside his robe for the Beretta.

Obviously satisfied that he was alone, Maimun bent down and thrust his fingers into the cobbled street. Tugging fiercely, he lifted a section of the alley floor. Barely defined in the weak moonlight, a black square opened up at the Arab's feet. Without wasted movement Maimun knelt and climbed inside, lowering the secret door quickly and firmly behind him.

James marked time by the beating of his heart. He hit the transmit button on the headset. "Rafael. Gary."

"Go," Encizo's calm voice came back.

"Our man just took a powder, guys," James said. "Approximately sixty yards into the alley, along the east wall, there's a hatch of some kind. Probably leads to a sewer under the city."

"Not necessarily," Encizo replied. "This city has been the site of religious wars for hundreds of years. It's possible that entrance leads to secret passages built under different sections of Jerusalem during the occupation of whatever warring faction was in power."

"Either way," James said grimly, "I'm going in after him. Don't know if these headsets will carry that far. Could be putting a lot of rock between you and me real quick."

"If we lose contact," Manning said, "that'll be me and Rafael closing the back door behind you."

"Right."

"Just take care of yourself down there, buddy. The numbers are tight enough now without losing you."

"I'll be sure to keep that in mind." James cleared the frequency and clicked the headset onto standby so that it would beep when a reception came in rather than take chances with an odd burst of static that could give him away.

With catlike silence he crossed the alley and knelt in the same spot where he'd seen Maimun disappear. His fingertips found the fissure in the cobblestones before he saw it. Once he'd found it, it was easy to see.

A straight line cut through the cobblestones, artificed so that the gap was less than an eighth of an inch. There was nothing even vaguely resembling a handle.

James reasoned Maimun had brought some kind of handle with him. And since the gap was so narrow, he also figured the door was counterweighted so that whatever was used wouldn't have to be very strong.

Taking a garrote wire from his pocket, the Phoenix Force warrior flattened one of the rings with the butt of the Beretta, then slipped it down between the gap. The flattened ring caught on the second pull. He slid back away from the opening, took a fresh grip on the pistol, hoped Maimun hadn't locked the door behind him and pulled.

The hatch swung up easily.

James extended the pistol into the tunnel's mouth, hammer eared back and his fingers resting lightly on the trigger.

Nothing moved.

Aware that even the moonlight streaming into the tunnel below could give him away, James slid inside without further hesitation. Iron rungs, rough and angular except where hands had worn them smooth over hundreds of years, were mortised into the uneven brick wall. They vibrated under James's weight but held him easily.

With the Beretta still in his right hand he flailed the other upward, caught the handle under the door and pulled it down. It closed with a shush and left him in darkness.

For a moment he remained still. During the brief time the door had been open, he hadn't glimpsed the tunnel's bottom. A methodical drip reached his ears. Musty vegetable odors took away all other smells and made the air seem thick. Something rustled ahead of him, but he couldn't be sure if it was someone or just the wind moving.

He cursed silently to himself and continued the descent. Three rungs later he stood on the uneven floor. Dust sifted underfoot. He judged the ceiling of the tunnel to be somewhere near nine feet in height.

The floor gradually dipped near the center of the tunnel, and the dust turned to thick mud. The tunnel was less than eight feet wide. James touched the other side after moving only a couple of steps.

He paused, not knowing whether to go forward or backward, and wondering where the hell Maimun had disappeared to. Having no other choice, he reached into his robe and pulled out a lighter. The radio was working perfectly now. He didn't want to take chances with his connection to Encizo and Manning. Maimun was the only lead Phoenix Force had left to the terrorist cell.

He thumbed the lighter to life and heard the movement to his left too late to react. The spark caught, ignited the wick and the yellow-and-blue flames arced up to fill the subterranean corridor with muzzy light and nightmarish shadows.

Calvin James got a brief impression of the big man standing beside him, then everything turned black again when the Arab swept the buttstock of an AK-47 across his face.

HAL BROGNOLA UNWRAPPED a fresh cigar and stuck it into a corner of his mouth. At his desk the President punched the replay button again. The news footage of Hamoud Jaluwi that had been enhanced through the computer at Stony Man Farm spun through the videocassette heads and displayed the picture on the television across the room.

It was the sixth time they'd watched the piece. It hadn't gotten any more palatable.

"The Russians," the Man said dispiritedly.

"Yes, sir," Brognola responded. "Maybe it's not as bad as we think. It could be Zagladin's operating from a lone branch of Directorate Thirteen."

"Do you think that's what it is?"

Brognola sighed, then answered honestly. "No."

"Neither do I." The President sat forward in his chair abruptly. "And, by God, I don't intend to tolerate this kind of behavior from them." He thumbed an intercom switch. "Katy."

"Yes, Mr. President?"

The Man glanced at his watch. "It's 3:17 p.m now. I want an audience with the Joint Chiefs of Staff at four o'clock."

"Yes, sir." The intercom went dead.

"Hal," the President said in disgust, "do you know the kind of problems this will cause on the international scene if it becomes public knowledge?"

"It's going to look like one big mud-slinging fight on the floor of the United Nations," Brognola said. "Iraq and Syria are both accusing the United States of being a country backing international assassinations. If we start crying foul against Russian involvement over there—when we're the only ones who're convinced it's going on, and all we have is a tape we've had computer-enhanced—we're going to look like we're only trying to save our own asses."

"Agreed. But I'll be damned if I let them break the rules without bending a few of my own. This puts us on a stricter time frame than we'd imagined, Hal."

Brognola nodded in agreement.

"If we could have only stayed the course on this engagement," the President said, "I feel certain our victory over Iraq and these terrorists would be only a few short months away. With the Soviets involved, who can say?"

Walking to the window, Brognola opened the shades enough to peer out at the afternoon sunshine falling over the green escarpment surrounding the White House. The bulletproof glass made things look slightly darker. Dozens of dump trucks loaded with sand and gravel lined the roads leading to the mansion proper. It was impossible to approach the White House in a vehicle without going through the zigzags created by the placement of the trucks. After the attack on Beirut in 1983 by terrorists, the same tactic had been employed by the Secret Service to prevent a suicidal terrorist from driving up into the nation's capital with enough explosives to leave nothing standing.

Siege mentality, the head Fed thought grimly, and the White House was indicative of the whole nation. Americans loved the idea of being the world protector, of being the defender. For the first time in fifty years, however, *defender* was a term that described the United States itself rather than the services the country offered because they were losing so much on home ground.

He turned to face the President. "There's something we can do."

"I'm listening."

"We can call the Soviets on this. Right now they have their anonymity as their first line of defense. If we take that away, convince them we're ready to get down in the dirt and play hardball with them, they might take a new tack on the whole situation."

"They won't willingly pull out."

"Nope. That's too much to hope for. But if we can put enough pressure on, we can buy ourselves, and this country, some time."

The President removed his glasses and rubbed at his bloodshot eyes tiredly. "Damn it. Buying time is a piss-poor objective in an operation where the stakes are this high."

"Yes, sir, but it might be the only positive move open to us at this time."

"How do you propose to set this up?"

"A meet between our representatives and theirs."

"Where?"

"The only neutral ground we've got where active martial players in this situation can meet," Brognola said. "Baghdad."

"You mean Striker?"

Brognola nodded.

"You're asking him to be very trusting to an extremely devious enemy."

"The final say-so will be his," Brognola said. "If he feels uncomfortable with it, he can scrub it at any time."

"Asking him to take part in this is like asking him to stick his head in a lion's mouth."

"There's the possibility the Soviets will deny all of this and turn us down flat. It could be we won't even have to ask him because they refuse."

The President was silent for a long moment. "All right, Hal, you've sold me. Striker's a good choice for this because he's not a politician. He won't mince words, and he'll know a line of bullshit when he smells it." He checked his watch again. "The first bombing raids are set to hit Baghdad in a little over twenty hours. It'll be 1700 hours their time. Striker can use that as his calling card. I'll get a call started through Soviet channels."

Brognola nodded. Yeah, Striker could use the bomb run as his calling card, the Fed reflected grimly, provided the big warrior found a safe haven during the time those bombs fell.

A BURST OF STATIC filled Gary Manning's ears as he sat tense and ready in the back seat of the Dodge Phoenix had recruited for their mission. He glanced at Encizo in the rearview mirror and saw by the concerned expression on his teammate's face that the Cuban was listening to the same thing.

"Shit," Manning said. He grabbed the silenced Heckler & Koch MP-5 SD-3 from the floorboard, slung an equipment pack over his shoulder and pushed out of the car.

Encizo, similarly equipped with an H&K machine pistol and pack, was a silent shadow two steps behind him.

Manning ran with the H&K MP-5 SD-3 in both hands and canted across his chest. He changed the ear-throat headset to the backup frequency on the operation. The static died away. There was no doubt in his mind that Calvin James had run into trouble.

Dressed in black camous, both men were hard to spot in the darkened alley. Manning wore a Beretta 92-F in a hip holster connected to the full battle webbing strung over his body. In the car he'd perspired and chafed under the Kevlar body armor. Now he was glad he had it.

"The alley's empty," Encizo said.

"Check," Manning responded. He glanced at his partner and saw that the smaller man had strapped on the night vision goggles from his pack. Straining his eyes, the big Canadian searched for the secret passageway Calvin James had told them about. Nothing turned up. "Do you see—"

"There." Encizo pointed.

Reaching into his pack, Manning pulled on his NVGs. The black staining the alley went away, colored instantly with a variety of greens. A moment later he spotted what Encizo had seen—a rectangle with too-straight borders backlit by pale green fire.

"I've got your back," Encizo transmitted. "You get the door."

Manning slung the machine pistol over his shoulder and dropped to the ground beside the hidden door. Closer now, he could see the wavering light change through the narrow gap left by the door. Using his combat knife, he probed for hinges until he found them.

"No matter how we handle this," Manning said as he sorted through his demolitions equipment, "once we prop this door, they're going to know we're coming. I figure if we've got surprise on our side, Calvin might live just a little longer."

"Agreed," Encizo said without hesitation. "You remove the door. I'm first man through, and I'm dropping straight to the bottom. Can't be that far. You back the play from up here."

"You got it. You just say when." Manning crammed a line of C-4 plastic explosive along the gap in the hidden door that housed the hinges, then affixed an electronic detonator. "When this goes, it's going to be smoking like the blazes. You want to watch the residual fire as you drop."

"Got it. Do it."

Manning thumbed the detonator, and a line of brilliant fire scorched the night. Metal creaked under the intense heat. Looking away from the explosion, Manning slid the H&K MP-5 SD-3 from his shoulder and took it up in both fists, his finger sliding through the trigger guard.

Moving without hesitation, Encizo leaped onto the hidden door framed by the fire left over by the C-4. With an agonized wrench the cobblestone-covered square ripped free of its moorings and dropped. Encizo dropped with it.

On his belly, using his elbows to navigate, Manning crawled to the hole in the alley and thrust the muzzle of the machine pistol inside. The NVGs lit up the interior of the tunnel.

Seven men scattered for cover below as Encizo landed among them. Manning squeezed the trigger in a controlled burst that took the man standing over Calvin James's prone form in the chest. The terrorist went back as the 9 mm parabellums chopped him down.

Still on the move, Encizo stretched out into a roll to lessen his impact against the floor. His machine pistol spit rapid whispers that took down two more Arabs.

"Calvin," Encizo said.

"I see him," Manning replied.

Encizo came up out of his roll with mud plastered across his back.

One of the terrorists traced a line of autofire across the ceiling of the tunnel with an AK-47, closing in on Manning's position. The Canadian unleashed a burst that removed the top of the man's head. The corpse banged back solidly against the far wall.

In motion already, obviously deciding his fate was a foregone conclusion, one of the remaining Arabs threw himself at James. A pistol gleamed in his fist.

Manning's stomach clenched in bitter frustration. At close range the H&K's bullets would rattle through the terrorist and hit James.

The ex-SEAL's left arm came up in a sweeping arc. Instantly all coordination seemed to leave the terrorist. The gun went off harmlessly, blowing a hole in the layer of mud covering the floor. Sparks flew in the wake of its passage.

Even with the NVGs turning everything a ghastly green, Manning could see the terrorist's slitted throat pumping blood. He slung the H&K subgun and lowered himself through the opening as Encizo dropped the remaining man. "Where's Maimun?"

Encizo kicked over a body and scanned the face. "I didn't see him."

"I didn't look," Manning admitted. "Katz would have my ass if I blew up our last lead."

"Maimun's not here," James said. He reached down into the mud and came up with his Beretta. "Man took a powder with two other guys when the door blew." He brushed the mud off the pistol, checked the action and found it satisfactory.

"Which way?" Encizo rummaged in his pack and brought out a pair of NVGs and an ear-throat headset for James.

"East." James slid into his gear.

Manning took the point, changing magazines in the subgun as he ran down the tunnel.

"I read this as a trap," Encizo transmitted. "If we miss Maimun here, I don't think we'll find anything helpful in this place. If he escapes, he'll vanish for good."

"I know," Manning said. The greenish pallor covering the walls of the tunnel bounced crazily in his restricted periphery as he lengthened his stride. Encizo and James splashed through the muck behind him. For a moment he didn't think he'd heard it because of the hum of the receiver in his left ear and the sound of Encizo and James bringing up the rear. He listened intently, found the thread of noise tangled up with all the others and followed it in his mind. "They're just ahead of us," he reported softly. "I hear the bastards now."

Breath searing his lungs, his mud-caked boots making his movement heavy and lethargic, Manning rounded a narrow twist in the tunnel. Even as he cleared the mouth of the tunnel he realized the running ahead of them had stopped.

Backlighted in emerald, three figures faced them in the narrow confines of the subterranean passage. One of them was halfway up a back wall, working at an overhead latch with frenzied desperation.

"Down!" Manning yelled. He threw himself forward and down, arms forward to take the brunt of the impact. Losing Encizo and James somewhere behind him, he skidded through the mud, sending layers of it peeling forward in spattering waves that covered his face and NVGs.

Autofire lit up the tunnel. Sparks burst from areas where bullets whined off the brick walls. Sharp stone splinters rained down.

Ignoring the pain of brick fragments striking his exposed face, Manning peered through the mud-filmed goggles and swept the H&K across the two Arab gunmen. Neither of them was Maimun.

The 9 mm burst crunched into them and blew them backward. Maimun had the door open and was frantically hoisting himself up.

Shifting the subgun to his left hand, Manning drew his Beretta and fired a single shot. Maimun's body arched in pain, then his struggles ceased. He fell back into the tunnel with outstretched arms and lay unmoving.

James flanked Manning's move toward the three terrorists. It only took a heartbeat to ascertain that both men were dead.

"We needed Maimun alive," Encizo said as he brought up the rear.

Manning peered down at the terrorist, then nudged him with a foot. "Old Maimun's alive," he said with a grin. "He's just playing possum. Aren't you, dude?"

Maimun's eyes flickered open, glaring hate at his captors. He spit, the effort partially wasted by the mud covering one side of his face, and missed.

"I never met a man," Manning said, reaching down to yank the terrorist to his feet, "who died from getting shot in the ass."

Hobbling painfully, Maimun said nothing. The right side of his butt bled profusely.

"You could have shot him in the foot," James said.

Manning shook his head. "I figured he might have made it if I put a bullet in an arm or a leg. And I couldn't miss that big ass even in the dark."

"True," Encizo said when he came over to join them. "But at least if you'd shot him in the arm or leg, he could have bandaged himself."

James grinned. "The way I see it, Gary, you shot him, so it's only fair you get to dress him out."

Manning stared at the terrorist and holstered his side arm. "Terrific."

7

Mack Bolan hurled himself from the belly of the C-130. The slipstream buffeted him unmercifully, bringing him perilously close to the body of the transport plane. Then it was gone. Thirty thousand feet below, the landscape was lost to view in the sable covering of night. Clad in black paratrooper's coveralls, he knew he'd be easily lost against the night.

Over a hundred pounds of gear was strapped to his body, including the air tanks necessary to make the high-altitude, high-opening drop. His face mask fogged each time he breathed out.

He glanced over his shoulder and saw the big Hercules transport craft veer off. A line of parachutists were spilled out behind it. With the coveralls masking her figure and straightening out the feminine curves, the Executioner only recognized Talia Alireza because she'd been the second jumper out the hatch.

"That's the lot of them," Jack Grimaldi radioed from the transport plane's cockpit. "I think everybody cleared."

"They did," Bolan radioed back. Glancing at the altimeter on his wrist, the warrior pulled the parachute release ring. Silk crackled over his head, jerking him out of the facedown starfish posture he'd been plunging earthward in. He grabbed the elevator controls and looked up at the rectangular shape spread above him.

"I'll see you at the rendezvous at 0500 hours," Grimaldi said. "Make sure your people are on time. From the latest intel I saw back at Kuwait City, the Iraqi air force controls most of the airspace between here and Baghdad."

"They'll be on time," Alireza transmitted in a professional rebuke.

"Understood, Valkyrie. No foul intended."

"No foul taken," she responded.

Bolan adjusted the chute, tracking into the correct direction. The target site was almost eighteen miles distant. From everything Eldridge and his people had discovered about the communications outpost, top-notch electronics had gone into it. But no matter how sophisticated the radar was, it wouldn't register the thirty parachutists closing in on its perimeters.

"A simple hit-and-git for your team, G-Force," Bolan reminded. "If everything goes as planned, we'll have the information ready for burst transmission when you're within range. Picking us up is secondary to the primary mission. If necessary, we'll find our own way home. Understood?"

"Affirmative, Striker."

"Take care, flyboy."

"Roger. Good hunting, people."

The C-130 banked and streaked east, back toward Kuwait City. The two F-14s riding shotgun kicked in their jets to keep up.

Bolan changed radio frequencies to the one used during the mission's drop. Once they reached the ground another frequency would be used. "By the numbers, people. I want to make sure we're all together. One."

"Two," Alireza counted off.

"Three," Jimoh transmitted.

The count continued until it hit thirty.

Satisfied, Bolan returned his full attention to the drop. With the chute acting like a hang glider, it was simple to keep on course. He alternated checking his watch, altimeter and the compass slung around his neck.

Besides the Desert Eagle .44 Magnum riding on his right hip and the Beretta in its customary shoulder leather, the Executioner was togged out in full war gear. The combat harness was heavy with incendiaries, spare magazines for his weapons and pouches containing spare rounds for the M-203 grenade launcher mounted under the M-16 he'd chosen as a lead weapon for the insertion. The rest of the assault team had been similarly equipped with M-16s and Beretta 9 mm side arms.

Talia Alireza's mercenaries had shown true professionalism when presented with the weaponry. There had been no complaints or hesitation. Each man had taken his assigned weapons, then immediately fieldstripped and cleaned them. It was immediately apparent they were familiar with the equipment.

Bolan adjusted the tracking, zooming down on the target zone only a few moments away now.

Alireza's voice was a surprise. "Good luck on the ground, Striker."

"You, too," he replied. He didn't look up to see the woman. There wasn't any time. Already the fortifications surrounding the communications output were becoming visible. Mounds of sandbags created strong defensive positions along the natural contours of the landscape. Sand-colored camou netting covered a handful of jeeps with machine gun mounts. Other machine gun emplacements were scattered throughout the area.

Eldridge's security people didn't have any intel regarding the defensive capabilities of the outpost. But with the Russians in the picture now, the Executioner had upgraded his estimate of the systems they'd be facing.

He tracked the parachute again and headed for a depression about five hundred yards from the first visible perimeter of the output. He thumbed the headset. "The LZ is on me. We move out on my mark. Squadron leaders will check in the moment your teams are on the ground and mobile."

Six affirmatives followed.

Bolan gathered his legs up, prepared to touch down after he spilled the air from the chute and thought for an instant that they were going to make the target area without incident.

Then the harsh, rattling bark of a .50-caliber machine gun lit up the night with orange tracers. Other gun emplacements joined the first.

The Executioner hit the ground with the knowledge that the target area had just become a hellzone. He rolled, shrugged out of the parachute harness and shouldered the M-16 while he raced to the top of the nearest sandy ridge to offer cover fire for the mercs still trapped in the air.

CARL LYONS MOVED restlessly through the thronging crowd who'd come to see the presidential campaign speakers. His cop's instinct chafed constantly, drawing familiar cold prickling between his shoulders. He knew that the same sour look he saw on the faces of the more experienced Washington, D.C., cops was plastered over his own features.

Rosario Blancanales's words in his ear over the headset only confirmed it. "Hey, Ironman, you look like you just swallowed a lemon."

"I'm thinking."

"Must be awful damn painful," Leo Turrin offered.

Lyons didn't even feel like searching for a retort. Things were so depressing at this point that he didn't have the energy. "You guys been approached by the press since we got here?"

"Not me," Gadgets said. Blancanales and Turrin followed suit. On their private channel they didn't have to worry about being overheard by the Soviet Service people and local law enforcement assigned to provide protection for the presidential debate.

More than two thousand people had gathered in Lafayette Square to hear the presidential hopefuls dodge questions concerning rising taxes, the protection of the American worker in the international marketplace and other concerns that had been dodged and lied about for a decade and more.

Two tables and a speaker's podium had been arranged at the foot of the equestrian statue of Andrew Jackson. The local blues had established perimeters of a sort, using red-and-white-striped sawhorses that were virtually useless. With everything under the heading of a political showcase, no one was being turned away.

"Guy came to me from one of the tabloids," Lyons said, glancing back over the crowd, "and offered me a chance on a pot some of the reporters were getting together for today's show."

"What kind of pot?" Blancanales asked.

"On when the terrorist attack would come and which candidate would go down first." Lyons cleaned his aviator-style sunglasses, which seemed to be as much a badge of office for the Secret Service men as their ID, on his shirttail and put them back on. He was dressed casually, with a windbreaker identifying him as Security in white letters across the back. The Government Model Colt .45 was snugged in breakaway shoulder leather. Able Team had more weapons stashed in the full-size Ford van parked with the police vehicles on Madison Place near the Pennsylvania Avenue exit.

"How much were the chances?" Schwarz asked.

"Forget it," Blancanales broke in. "All the good times are probably already taken. They're just looking to bump up the table stake with latecomers."

"Personally," Schwarz said, "I've been in the money more on long shots than on sure things."

Realizing Schwarz and Blancanales were about to launch into one of their familiar arguments, Lyons tapped the Tach Two frequency used by the locals' officer corps into the headset. Schwarz, Turrin or Blancanales could beep him if they wanted his attention.

Lyons continued threading his way through the outskirts of the crowd. His gut told him the attack, when it came, would come from the outer perimeters. Even with the mixture of skin tones inside Lafayette Park, it would be hard to insinuate terrorist gunmen inside the cordoned-off area. The first gunshot would set off a panic that would make further attacks against the candidates useless.

But then, he reasoned, to be successful all the terrorists had to do was kill as many of the people around them as they could.

Guarding them all was an impossibility.

"Seems hopeless, doesn't it?" Leo Turrin asked.

Lyons turned and found the stocky Fed closing in on him, holding two cups in his hands.

"Am I that obvious?"

Turrin passed a soft drink over. "Ironman, if they could just broadcast the dark looks in your eyes to every man, woman and child gathered here, everybody'd be home right now." Like Lyons, Turrin was dressed casually, black windbreaker fluttering loosely around him.

Lyons drank the soda pop gratefully. "All I need now is a hot dog. Then the afternoon would be set for wholesale slaughter."

"Now there's a warming thought," Turrin said.

"You were a cop. You know just as well as I do how the percentages work on these things."

Turrin nodded. "I never worked out in the open like you did. Some of this is new, but a lot of the feelings are the same. Feels a lot like being on a roller coaster bound straight for hell. I know what you mean about the news guys now," Turrin went on. "I passed a couple of them who were doing comparison figures on the number of victims at each of the candidate hits so far. Seems they've started their own poll, counting each death as a vote. When I left, they were speculating on how well our two guys up there would do today."

Lyons shook his head wordlessly. He was accustomed to the callousness often displayed by professionals who dealt in death and dying every day. But he didn't condone it. Not when he could look out into the crowd and see the number of kids dragging helium-filled campaign balloons through the open area of the park.

"Something's up," Turrin said quietly. He raised a hand to adjust the headset frequency. "Tach One."

Lyons beeped Blancanales and Schwarz, dropped in on their loop long enough to alert them to the situation, then switched to Tach One himself.

The communications net was filled with fast-breaking reports.

"Dispatch, this is Fifty-Four rolling on the Farragut North station squeal."

"Roger, Fifty-Four. What is your ETA?"

"Two minutes, Dispatch."

"Affirmative, Fifty-Four. Be advised that an unconfirmed caller has reported shots fired. Be on the lookout for at least three armed men of possible Middle Eastern extraction.''

Lyons looked at Turrin. ''Farragut North?''

Grim-faced, Turrin nodded. ''Subway station. Block, block and a half away from here.''

Lyons beeped for Blancanales and Schwarz, switched to the Able Team frequency, then hit the transmit button. ''Did you copy that?''

''Roger,'' Blancanales replied. ''I'm moving on it now.''

''Ditto,'' Schwarz said.

Lyons moved back onto the Tach Two frequency knowing the rest of Able Team would, too. Unit commanders were bellowing orders to their squadron commanders. An effort to move the audience and the speakers to the southeast quarter of Lafayette Park, away from Connecticut Avenue and K Street, began to take shape.

The people moved slowly, whether held in place by confusion or by anticipation, Lyons wasn't sure. Moving at a run, glancing back toward the northwest where Farragut North subway station was, he unlimbered the .45. Schwarz and Blancanales would be moving on their vehicle now, breaking out the heavier armament Able Team had brought to the site.

Police vehicles from Madison Place were in motion now. With swirling cherries and frenetic bleats from the sirens, they plowed up over the curbs and charged toward the northwest corner of the park.

Lyons intercepted a young police officer yelling orders to the audience through a bullhorn. The officer's amplified voice sounded calm, as if the whole episode were just a fire drill.

''Laramie,'' Lyons identified himself as he reached for the bullhorn. ''I'm with the Justice Department. I need to borrow this.''

The policeman allowed it to be taken from his hand.

Keying up the bullhorn, Lyons held his .45 a few inches from the speaker, then pulled off three rapid shots. The rounds sounded like explosions going off over the park area. The last *crack* overloaded the bullhorn and broke the speaker. But the crowd got the message and moved from a walk into a full-fledged run.

Lyons shoved the bullhorn back into the surprised policeman's hands without a word. He gazed after the crowd, feeling defeat gather around him because it had had to be this way. The audience had become a mob, spurred on by self-survival. He knew people were going to be hurt by his actions, but also knew those same actions might have saved lives, too.

Uniformed policemen fell into the crowd, trying to give direction toward East Executive Avenue. A river of flesh and blood poured out onto Pennsylvania Avenue, stopping traffic with a skidding and shrieking of tortured rubber and human fear.

As Lyons watched the confusion roiling over into the street, he realized the SWAT teams and Secret Service people had to put an end to the terrorist threat here. Otherwise, anyone getting through the park would have a street full of targets to choose from directly in front of the White House. All forward momentum on part of the park crowd was stalling out and dying in the street.

Lyons kept his pistol high and in front of him as he cut through the crowd and worked his way toward the threatened area. The news choppers buzzed lower, fighting one another for airspace to shoot footage. Flocks of startled pigeons created even more havoc.

Police cars streaking in from Connecticut Avenue signaled the arrival of the terrorists. The thunderous cracks of high-calibered weapons wiped away the last trace of normal city sounds.

The terrorists were a human wave that washed over the edge of the park, held at bay only for a moment by the outer perimeter established by the police, then rushed on through.

Lyons had his pistol up, firing as soon as he had a clear target. He couldn't count the number of terrorists but figured somewhere near thirty. American law-enforcement personnel outnumbered them, but the sheer ferocity and determination of the terrorists gave them a momentum that seemed irresistible.

Ironman determined to be the immovable object. He took a wide-legged stance and fished for a fresh magazine while he fired the .45 dry with the other hand. Bullets plucked at him, tearing splinters from the park bench and trees beside him.

One of his targets took a round in the chest and went spinning less than twenty feet away. Before Lyons could reload, the terrorist immediately following the other man was on him. Unwilling to give ground, Lyons met his attacker head-on.

The terrorist's speed and weight knocked them both off balance. The man screamed and tried to bring his Uzi to bear.

Lyons lost the .45 somewhere in the scuffle and felt the air burst out of his lungs as they hit the ground. The Uzi's forward sight raked his forehead and spilled blood into his eyes. He blinked them clear, raised a forearm to smash against the terrorist's face, but lost the man when the guy went rolling back with the blow.

Rolling over on his right side, Lyons twisted his wrist and freed the .45 Semmerling Derringer from its spring-out rig. The little gun fitted smoothly into his palm. He squeezed off two rounds, which cored the terrorist's face.

On his feet, breath starting to fill his lungs again, Lyons found the .45. He changed magazines and scanned the confusion around him, only then aware that the law enforcement people had held the line.

The sparse gunfire died away entirely. While other men closed in on their fallen assailants, Lyons checked the two men he'd downed. Both were dead. He glanced around.

A haze of blue-gray cordite smoke drifted across Lafayette Square. The irregular line of police cars fronting the street showed bullet holes and damage done by grenades. Lyons only then remembered the concussions going off around him. Plainclothes cops, uniformed officers and SWAT members dressed in black lay among their enemy where they'd fallen. Some screamed in mortal agony.

Lyons's headset beeped. He switched to the Able Team frequency, automatically scanning the bloody expanse of park for his comrades-in-arms. "Go."

In the distance ambulances roared onto the scene, pulling immediately from the streets onto the park grounds.

"Got some bad news, Ironman," Blancanales said.

Lyons found Pol near Gadgets. They were kneeling over a third man. "What?"

"Leo took a bullet," Blancanales told him, "and I don't know if he's getting up from this one."

BUTTSTOCK OF HER WEAPON fitted smoothly against her cheek, Talia Alireza took aim on her target and squeezed off a 3-round burst.

The Iraqi soldier had been taking cover behind a sandbag wall. The 5.56 mm tumblers caught him in the side and pitched him out into the open.

Her next burst zipped the man from chest to throat and spilled his corpse onto the thirsty desert sand. Alireza didn't glance over her shoulder to see how the rest of her team was doing despite her intense desire to do so. Looking away, even to make sure they were making it to ground safely, might cost a life.

The Iraqi machine gun nests filled the night air with orange tracer fire. Sand whipped up in front of Alireza as a continuous burst raced across the sand dune she was using for cover. Her vision blurred by tears from the sand in her eyes, she refused to give up, moving onto the next target.

The sound of whining engines reached her ears. She glanced toward the motor pool in time to see the first of the jeeps pull out.

Readying the M-203 mounted under the American assault rifle, she rubbed her shirtsleeved forearm across her eyes, then took aim at the machine gun nest nearest her. The distance was just over one hundred yards, well within the range of the weapon. She took up the trigger slack and felt the kick as the 40 mm warhead took flight.

A heartbeat later it landed slightly off-center in the gun emplacement. The explosion blew the gun crew out of the sandbagged fortification and tore the walls down. Only one man appeared to be left alive, but a single round from the M-16 settled that.

The headset clicked in her ear, then Bolan's voice came to her, calm and clear. "Squadron leaders, report in."

A jeep raced for the high road, profiled against the dark bulk of the sand dune behind it. The vehicle slid for a moment, losing traction, then a 40 mm grenade landed near it and sent the jeep tumbling in fiery wreckage end over end down the incline.

Alireza reported in as squadron leader when her time came. The remainder of her clip was spent picking off stragglers who'd survived the grenade she'd launched into the machine gun emplacement. She changed magazines. Instinctively she registered the fact that only Squadrons One and Four were completely intact. As leader of Squadron Two, she'd lost two men, leaving her operating abilities at something over sixty percent. It took an effort of will not to wonder who'd been taken out of the play. For now they had to be pieces in the game, not men.

"Squadrons One and Three," Bolan said, "will move out on my mark and breach the outer perimeters of the target zone. Ready, Three?"

Jimoh answered without hesitation. "Ready, One."

"Mark," Bolan ordered.

Twelve men surged up from the ground like a wave of human flesh cresting the sand dune.

Alireza couldn't identify them. She knew their names because she'd helped draw up the groups. Leaning into her weapon, she took control of the three squadrons left behind, ordering Five to see to the wounded that were in danger of becoming casualties.

She bracketed the face of another Iraqi soldier in her sights. He was young, intense, almost skilled as he brought his assault rifle up to fire. For a moment her mind wandered, prodded her imagination into believing that the man in front of her had once been a boy she might have played with as a child when she still lived in Baghdad. She had difficulty pulling the trigger. But she did, then moved onto the next target.

It felt as if some small piece of herself had died with the young man.

DAVID MCCARTER UNCOILED from the driver's seat of his car and let himself quietly out into the night. His body ached from hours spent cramped inside the vehicle. He'd had nothing to eat since morning because he'd been unwilling to leave Katz unattended.

Phoenix Force's leader had been spared the privilege of being taken to any of the government buildings downtown. His Mossad captors had installed him, instead, at a leather goods factory west of Ben Yehuda Street on Jaffa Road. The agents had taken Katz in during the height of the business day, but no one appeared to notice. It had given McCarter the idea that it wasn't the first time the factory had been used to house prisoners the Mossad didn't want others to know about.

In addition to the Browning Hi-Power leathered under his left arm, McCarter carried an Ithaca Model 37 12-gauge pump shotgun on a Whipit shoulder sling under his right arm. He wore a charcoal-gray duster whose end fluttered at the calves of his leg and concealed the hardware. Leaving his right arm out of the duster's sleeve bought him precious seconds he'd need once he kicked the opening numbers into play.

Two sentries covered the perimeters of the leather factory. From their synchronized movements McCarter had deduced they were the usual night watch employed by the company.

And they were good. The first man actually heard McCarter coming before the Briton could completely close the gap. Stationed by the alley entrance that had double doors beside it to service truck deliveries and shipments, the man's face was a pale oval in the darkness.

The guy turned and raised his Uzi to fire.

Moving briskly, McCarter clapped his left palm over the guard's gun hand, tripping the fire selector all the way back to the safety position before they guy could squeeze off a round. Then he brought his free arm up in a vicious elbow blow that slammed the Mossad agent's head against the brick wall behind him.

The thud sounded meaty, painful. Unconscious immediately, the guard slumped forward.

McCarter caught the man, then dragged him into the shadows lining the delivery bay doors. He rested his fingers against the guard's exposed neck. The pulse fluttered but remained strong. Satisfied he'd done no permanent damage, McCarter relieved the man of his Uzi, tossed the weapon and the pistol from a belt holster on top of the overhang above the loading area, then snapped a pair of plastic handcuffs into place.

He moved back to the regular doorway, conscious of the sounds around him. A pocket held an assortment of lockpicks in a plastic case. He let himself in through the locked door with an alacrity that would have shocked his old headmaster at Sandhurst Military Academy.

Once inside, he shrugged out of the duster and tossed it under the spindly legged shipping desk. His back pocket yielded a full-face watch cap. He slid it onto is head, leaving his face uncovered for the moment, not wanting to restrict his peripheral vision until he had no choice.

The Mossad knew Katz's face. That was one out of five. McCarter didn't intend to add to their mug file on Phoenix Force while they were still operating illegally in-country.

The docking bay opened up into the production-assembly room proper. The stark, still hunks of machinery lay dormant now, no buzz of sewing machines or thump of diecutters. Occasional security lights gleamed from the metal surfaces.

The production area was a large rectangle that had almost every available space filled with worktables and machinery. Above the floor, with metal stairs running up to it, was a row of offices. Yellow light outlined the third door down. There were no windows in the wall as there were in other offices.

McCarter's recon before moving into the factory hadn't revealed the lighted room, telling him the people inside had been careful about discovery.

Unseen, McCarter moved through the production floor and came to a stop under the outer ledge of the office floor. He reached up, caught the ledge in his gloved fingers and pulled himself up. Using the metal stairs would have caused more noise.

Moving along the catwalk in front of the offices, he heard voices coming from the lighted room. His hand slid around the Ithaca's grip and he slipped off the safety. At the door he listened for a moment. He didn't hear Katz, but he did hear at least three other men in the room.

The element of surprise was cut thin at times, and McCarter knew it. Still, when it was the only card a man had to play, he played it hard.

His fingers turned the watch cap down, covered his face and adjusted it. Standing in front of the door, he lifted the shotgun and aimed at the locking mechanism.

He squeezed the trigger, and the boom of the shotgun bellowed to life around him. The round tore the lock from the door, then the metal-ceramic projectile evaporated without penetrating.

McCarter racked the slide and strode into the room.

8

The M-16 ran dry in Mack Bolan's hands as he charged the communications post. The M-203 was already empty. Before he had the chance to change magazines an Iraqi soldier came around a wall of sandbags and locked his AK-47 to his shoulder less than eight feet away.

The Executioner ducked and felt one of the bullets plow along the Second Chance armor covering his back. Using textbook skill and the commitment to the mission that fired him, he drove the rifle bayonet into the Iraqi's chest. The warm, wet mist of the man's last living breath hissed against the warrior's face. Then the man was another corpse lying in the desert sand.

Bolan withdrew the bayonet and rammed a fresh clip into the M-16. There were fewer targets now. The merc force had driven the Iraqis back to the inner recesses of the outpost. Iraqi vehicles burned from the 40 mm grenades that had taken them out of action, and only three machine gun nests were still operational.

Hunkering down behind the sandbag wall, Bolan freed a grenade, pulled the pin with his teeth and lobbed it overhand. When the three-second fuse went, only two machine gun nests remained.

He was in motion at once, advancing into the sand and rock falling back down to earth. One of the Iraqi soldiers was still alive and reached for his weapon. A 3-round burst from the M-16 amended that.

Bolan tapped the transmit button on his headset. "Four, this is One. What's your situation?"

"One, this is Four. We have the back door secure. These people have nowhere to go."

"Acknowledged, Four. Move your people in slowly."

"Roger, One."

Bolan swiveled his field of view and caught the rolling dive one of the Iraqis made in an attempt to gain a defensive stance behind a natural wall of low rock. The Executioner waited, then flicked the selector on the assault rifle to single-fire. When the man's head came up to take stock of his position, Bolan put a 5.56 mm tumbler between the guy's eyes. He moved on, not waiting to watch the Iraqi fall.

"Two, this is One."

"Go, One."

"Your situation?"

"Stabilized." Talia Alireza's voice sounded strained.

"Our people?"

"I have four dead. Two of them never made it clear of their chutes."

Bolan didn't make a comment. That could come later. His questions now weren't generated by an emotional need to know. "Your wounded?"

"Stabilized, as well."

"How many players can you field?"

"Ten, at full speed. Three stragglers. And one will have to remain immobilized here."

"Affirmative, Two. The ten will be ready to set up security perimeters and establish a sky watch on my mark. No survivors. This is a clean kill."

"Roger, One."

Still on the move, Bolan let the NVGs light up the night for him. The land was level here and rolled right on through the camou-covered area where the main intelligence work of the communications post was done. Iraqi movement was limited to the motions of survival. Their position had been overrun, and they were good enough soldiers to know they were living on borrowed time.

Bolan threw himself over a sandbag wall and landed on his feet on the other side. Twenty feet from his position was another defensive post for gunners. He ripped a grenade from his combat harness and heaved it. The explosion flickered, then lit up the night.

His boots sank into the loose sand as he ran, moving into the defensive position. It was clean. He knelt and watched for a moment as his squadron's members, and Four's, systematically grenaded out all suspicious configurations in the sandbag walls. It was like taking a house, only instead of starting at the top and working down, the teams worked from the outside in.

Autofire coming from the main tent was more intense now. There was no way to estimate how many men might remain inside.

None of the grenades landed near the main tent. Bolan's orders had been specific about that. They'd make an effort to retrieve whatever intel was inside rather than destroy it.

Running again, Bolan closed the distance to the main tent to just under sixty yards. He tapped the transmit button on the headset. "Squadron One, this is One. Count off if you're mobile. One-one."

Four men counted off in quick succession.

"One-six, what's your situation?"

"I took a round, One-one. If the call's fast, I'm not your man."

"Affirmative, One-six. Can you cover?"

"Like frosting on a cake, One-one."

"I'm holding you to that, soldier."

"Yes, sir."

Bolan checked the main tent again. The autofire had slowed to brief crackles from slits cut in the camou material. "One-two, you're with me on my mark."

"Yes, sir."

"One-three, One-four?"

A double affirmative responded.

"Stun grenades," Bolan ordered, "again, on my mark. Put them within damage control radius of the tent. You will snipe in single-fire at known targets to cover myself and One-two."

The team radioed acknowledgment.

"Four, do you copy?" Bolan asked.

"Four copies." Jimoh's voice was resonant, ready.

Bolan keyed the transmit button again. "Two, do you copy?"

"Two copies."

Once he was hunkered down in a runner's starting position, Bolan said, "Grenades away."

"Grenades away, One-one."

A double thunderclap threw sizzling light only a few yards from the sandbag walls of the main tent. Sparks showered the camoued rooftop but didn't catch because the material was fire retardant.

"Mark, One-two," Bolan signaled as he threw himself from cover. He made long strides, keeping his weight distributed forward so that he could change and throw it in any direction if it became necessary. A lean shadow charged the tent beside him.

Covering fire rang out as single shots. Answering fire from the cornered Iraqi soldiers came in full, rattling roars.

The Executioner kicked off-stride as a line of 7.62 mm bullets raked slashes through the sand in search of him. Through the greenish haze presented by the NVGs he saw a bullet core through the tent material where the assault rifle poked out. The rifle dropped away.

He went down in a roll ten feet from the tent and came up using the sandbag walls for cover. He tapped the transmit button on the headset. "One-two, short bursts when we go in. Make certain of the kill."

"Affirmative, One-one." The merc sat curled up outside the second door facing out. His assault rifle was tight and ready in his fists.

"Plastique," Bolan instructed. He took a small amount of C-4 from his chest pack, rolled it into a four-inch tube and placed it along the door lock. He set the electronic detonator for five seconds, then slapped it into the explosive. "Eight seconds, One-two, on my mark." With the M-16 canted along his hip he freed two tear gas canisters and readied them for operation. "Gas goes in first. Quick four-count, then you follow it in."

"Understood, One-one."

Bolan dropped the NVGs near the sandbag wall. The exchange of fire was sporadic again. It wouldn't be long before someone inside the tent came out to brace them. "Two. Four."

Alireza and Jimoh checked in.

"I'll be out of touch for a bit. Back in the net as soon as I can."

"Roger, One," the woman confirmed.

"One-two, we're operational on hand signals inside. Anything moving after we blow the doors goes down."

"Understood, One-one."

Bolan took a last clear breath, tasting the dry freshness of the desert air. "Okay, Two, Four, move your squads in and make them nervous. See you people on the other side." He tossed the headset, pulled the gas mask over his head and fitted it into place. He signaled his accomplice with the M-16, then slammed the detonator into operation.

The rate of fire picked up dramatically. No one inside the tent seemed to notice grenades weren't being launched.

Five seconds later the door imploded. Without hesitation the Executioner tossed in his CS grenades. Even with the earlier blast ringing in his ears he heard their pops and hisses when they went off.

He went around the doorway low. A burst of gunfire raked over his head. The M-16 came up automatically, bracketed a twin burst on the shooter and spilled a corpse back against a sandbag wall.

The door leaned drunkenly on its wooden frame. The lock had been blown away, leaving a half-moon shape filled with sharp splinters.

The other door blew, spreading the billowing CS gas around inside. Hacking, coughing, gagging, sneezing and snuffling sounds echoed inside the tent. Corkboards covered the sandbag walls with pushpinned information. Five desks were heavily laden with electronic equipment. The merc team had left the generator intact at Bolan's order. Provided the communications outpost was computer-linked, Bolan wanted the systems up for stripping rather than chance losing a valuable lead.

The Executioner and the merc caught the Iraqi soldiers in a vicious cross fire that made instant casualties. Bolan guessed there were close to twenty men in the tent. Half of them escaped through slits they cut through the back of the tent, choosing a course that would bring them into direct contact with Jimoh and Squad Four, closing up the rear.

Someone had started a fire against the back wall on Bolan's side. There was no time to recharge the M-16. He unleathered the Desert Eagle and put two rounds into the Iraqi soldier who spun around to face him. The body fell forward into the flames and lay there.

Taking care but wasting no time, the Executioner crossed the crowded room. He stepped over two corpses. A penflash showed him the red fire extinguisher hanging from the sandbags. He glanced at the merc and gave the all-secure hand signal. The man flashed it back.

Keeping the .44 Magnum in his fist, Bolan used his other hand to grab the extinguisher and spew its contents over the flames burning atop the desk. Papers and embers blew everywhere, lost occasionally in the CS clouds trapped inside the command post.

Side arm in hand, the mercenary checked each of the nine men lying on the loose carpet overtop the sandy floor and gave them each an insurance round through the head.

The papers Bolan had rescued were in Arabic, and he couldn't read them. But there were enough maps of allied territory in Kuwait to let him know they were important. He grabbed them by the fistful and shoved them into his chest pack.

A solid ring of mercenaries met him when he stepped outside the post and took off the gas mask. He retrieved his headset and slid it on. There were no more gunshots. An uneasy silence had settled over the desert.

"Two," a voice called out.

"Go," Alireza responded.

"Four's down," the man said. "He's hit bad."

Already in motion, Bolan ran up the side of the hill that partly framed the main tent.

AN ORANGE JACK-O'-LANTERN followed the shotgun blast into the room. Still tied up in the chair where his Mossad interrogators had left him for the past few hours, Katz experienced a moment where he thought his senses were deceiving him. But the shotgun blast had been too real, and it would have awakened him from a dream even if he *had* been asleep.

Therefore he accepted the reality of the shotgun-brandishing jack-o'-lantern and tipped his chair over to get out of the way of gunfire and to make his escape. For the past two hours he'd been slowly working on the ropes that bound his hand and feet to the chair and had managed an interesting inch or two of slack that none of his captors had noted.

Four Mossad agents were scattered around the small office. The second explosion from the shotgun was deafening, merciless.

The man sitting on top of the desk went over backward, papers scattering in his wake. The microcassette recorder dropped to the floor and shattered.

The jack-o'-lantern pumped the slide and picked up a second target as the Mossad agent reached for the pistol in his shoulder harness. Now Katz could see that the jack-o'-lantern was really a ski mask pulled down over a man's face. The shotgun banged. Flailing from the impact, the second Mossad agent went down in a boneless heap against the far wall.

The wooden chair had weakened when it slammed against the floor. Katz strained against his bonds. The chair legs and back came apart and the rope loosened. Even with only one hand he had his bonds loosened in seconds.

The Phoenix Force leader rose to his feet as the third man targeted the jack-o'-lantern, who punched a third round into the fourth Mossad agent, leaving his back open to the remaining man.

Balanced on the ball of his foot at the side and slightly behind the last Mossad agent, Katz unleashed a powerful savage kick. His foot caught the man behind the jaw with crushing force and bounced him off the wall. The agent lost his weapon and came off the wall wide-eyed directly into a follow-up spinning back kick that knocked him senseless.

Katz wasted no time in retrieving a weapon. When he glanced back up, McCarter had rolled up the ski mask enough to reveal his face. The Briton thumbed replacement shells into his shotgun.

"What are you doing here?" Katz asked. He crossed the room and looked down at the nearest Mossad agent. There was no blood.

"Oh, don't worry, mate. They're still alive." McCarter picked up a blunt piece of PVC from the floor. "Used baton rounds on them. Figured it would either put them out or soften them up enough for us to work on them at our leisure."

Katz breathed a silent sigh of relief. Though enlisted on the same mission—more or less—though with different agendas, he didn't want Israeli blood on his hands. "You haven't answered my question."

"About my being here?" McCarter flashed him an innocent look.

"I gave specific instructions, David. You were told to forget about me and get on with the mission."

"It's been gotten on with, mate. You, however, were a loose end."

"The Israelis wouldn't have harmed me."

"Maybe they wouldn't have killed you," McCarter retorted, "but it looks as if they didn't hold back none when it came to the area of physical abuse."

The ache and sting of the bruises covering Katz's face and upper body felt like a second skin. His captors had been well schooled in the extraction of hidden truths, and they hadn't been hesitant about employing their training.

"What say we continue this invigorating little chat elsewhere?" McCarter asked.

Katz gathered two spare clips for the Beretta and shoved them into his pockets. He took point, letting the Briton bring up the rear.

"The others?" Katz asked.

"Working on the mission," McCarter replied.

"Have they had any success with Maimun?"

"Beats me, mate. I've been sitting outside in a car all day. I'm tired, I'm hungry and I've been shot at by professionals, mind you, and not one blessed word of thanks." Mc-Carter pointed out the door leading to the loading docks. "It's true I didn't expect any, but I didn't expect to get reamed for getting you out of there."

"You disobeyed an order, David. I told you to leave me where I was."

"Where you were," McCarter said, "was bloody well dangerous. To yourself and to the rest of Phoenix. You knew the specifics of our mission, knew the players involved and you knew how spread out the Stony Man forces are in the allied troop forces. I couldn't leave you in place because you knew too much. Sooner or later those people would have broken you to get at what you knew. You know that and I know that. Let's be adults here and not kid ourselves."

Katz passed through the loading docks and into the cool night air beyond. In seconds he was feeling much better. "And if you hadn't been successful in getting me out?"

McCarter regarded him from under the dark folds of the jack-o'-lantern mask without expression. "Why, I suppose I'd have shot you dead, mate."

They crossed the street, approached McCarter's car and got in. "Under the conditions," Katz said, "I suppose I shouldn't be too harsh on you for disobeying a direct order."

"Sign of a good soldier is to know when to take a command that hasn't exactly been given," McCarter said as he started the engine. "If you'd had more time to think about it, you'd have seen things the same way I did. If you don't think that's satisfactory, we can always go back up in that building and replay this hostage rescue situation with the alternative that the hostage doesn't get out alive."

"That won't be necessary." Katz tried to keep a sober expression on his face, but it fell short. A smile kept getting in the way.

"Didn't think so, mate." McCarter flashed him a cocky grin, slid his aviators into place and pulled smoothly out onto the street.

By the time McCarter had meshed with the other late-night traffic, Katz's mind was already involved with the rest of the mission, wondering what successes or calamities had befallen the rest of Phoenix.

TALIA ALIREZA'S HANDS warmed with Jimoh's blood as it poured out of his wounds. More of the red liquid seeped into her desert camous and soaked into the sand, turning it black. She held back her tears because she couldn't hold back the blood.

"Thought I had them," Jimoh said weakly. He coughed, then closed his eyes.

For a heartbeat Alireza didn't think the man would open them again. She held his head in her lap, trying to make him comfortable. He felt heavy against her, reassuring, as if he were there to stay, but she knew she was losing him. Two of the squad worked frantically around Jimoh with the first-aid kit, patched the wounds in his lower abdomen and sought to perform the impossible.

Jimoh's eyes blinked back open. The whites were incredibly stark except for the veins. "Took me off like a fuckin' greenhorn rookie." The man sighed, and a bubble of blood exploded against his lips and left a red stain.

"Take it easy." Alireza's voice was calm. "You're going to be okay."

A rictus twisted Jimoh's lips, and she knew the man was trying to smile. "Why do you want to lie to me, Talia, after all the years we've been working together?"

"Maybe I was lying to myself."

His hand came up, trembling in a way she'd never seen it do before. Once it had been so steady, a rock she could depend on when an operation was blown from the outset. She gripped his hand, found hers lost inside his, but immediately knew she was the stronger.

He licked his lips. "Don't blame yourself for this."

One of the soldiers working on Jimoh's wounds looked up and pushed his black helmet back with a bloodstained thumb. Wetness gleamed in his eyes, softening the hard lines of his face. He shook his head slowly.

Alireza gripped Jimoh's hand more tightly. There was no return pressure coming from his fingers.

"You hear me?" Jimoh asked. "I said don't blame yourself for this."

She nodded. "I hear you."

"Had to happen," Jimoh went on in a whisper. "Sooner or later, you live life on the edge the way we do, you're going to get cut. Haven't I always told you that?"

"Yes." Unable to hold them back any longer, tears spilled down her face.

"Just keep your head clear," Jimoh advised. "And maybe I was wrong."

She looked at him and felt him convulse in her grasp.

"Maybe I was wrong," he repeated, "about listening to your heart. Maybe, here and now in this place where you came from, maybe that's what you should be listening to. A lot of people are going to get hurt before this is over."

The two men who'd been tending Jimoh moved away.

Alireza watched them, then saw Bolan looming on the sandy incline behind the men like some dark specter. She held back her anger, feeling it line up to focus on the American. Her headset crackled in her ear. Part of her mind listened to the team setting up perimeter security.

"If you can," Jimoh said in a hoarse whisper, "don't leave me here. Send me home. Let me lie with the bones of my ancestors."

A lie caught in her throat as she started to tell him not to think about dying anymore. Instead she said, "You have my promise."

He gave her a crimson-stained smile. "There's worse things than dying, Talia."

"I know."

"Being lost is one of them." Jimoh swallowed the effort. "You've hidden from yourself too long." He sighed. "If this had never happened, maybe I would never have told you that. But now is the time. I feel it. You've been torn between your selves for too long. Find your dreams, and heal yourself. Give yourself part of that good life waiting out there."

She nodded, unable to speak.

A gentle calm descended over Jimoh, and he was gone.

Alireza wiped the tears from her eyes, placed the man's hand over his chest and got to her feet. When she looked back up the incline where Bolan had been standing, he was gone.

HEARING THE PING of the radio beacon when it came to life, Jack Grimaldi crushed his cigarette underfoot and reached for the Huey UH-1D's headset. He settled the communications gear into place, thumbed the ignition to life and scanned the other two helicopters through the Plexiglas windows. They sat in a loose circle facing each other, silent and deadly in the night's embrace.

He flicked the transmit button. "Okay, you bunch of heroes, it's show time." His hand slid smoothly around the control stick. Increasing the rotor speed, he let the big transport chopper take the air. Desert sand sprayed out around him, wafted back inside by confused crosscurrents.

He blinked it out of his eyes, then slid his protective goggles into place.

So far the radar sweeps had been clean despite the increased air activity along the Kuwait border stemming from Iraqi bases.

"Count off," Grimaldi ordered. "Over."

"Nighthawk One. We're operational, Nighthawk Leader. Over."

"Acknowledged, Nighthawk One. Over."

"Nighthawk Two. Operational, sir. Over."

"Roger, Nighthawk Two. Nighthawk Leader has the point. We play it by the book, gentlemen. You break out of formation *only* on my orders. Over."

"Affirmative, Nighthawk Leader. Over."

"Nighthawk Two understands, Nighthawk Leader. Over."

Grimaldi cleared the frequency. The three helicopters rose out of the dish-shaped area of desert like thunderous ghosts. A silver quarter moon hung above them, gave the sandy landscape a feeling of unreality and left stark shadows draped across the hills and valleys.

They flew nap-of-the-earth, easy prey for any ground-based troops they might encounter despite the armament they carried. Grimaldi felt the tension inside him, but refused to let it find an outlet in his reflexes while handling the Huey. His eyes and arm were part of the big machine. Scores of aerial combat had hardened his nerves to steel, giving them the lightning-fast reflexes of quicksilver. But the soul of the pilot still harbored its doubts and fears.

Still, the beacon was a good sign. It meant Bolan and his party were operational. At least some of them. Grimaldi was too conscious of the body bags lying in wait in the rear of the helicopter.

He cleared his mind of the negative thinking and focused on his responsibilities in the mission. All three Hueys were heavily armed, but combat ability wasn't a priority. The air-to-ground rockets and 7.62 mm machine guns were there to buy time, not avenge.

Glancing at the compass needle, he compared his findings to the reading from the beacon ping, then made the adjustments. The tail rotor spun the craft slightly to the left, away from the silvered moon.

He looked back over his shoulder. The other helicopters trailed him like dark shadows. Everything looked fine. Part of him relaxed. He glanced at the compass again, then checked his watch. With any kind of luck his team could be in and out of the target area within minutes.

Then the special communications gear linking him to the Stony Man Farm frequency lit up an amber light that let him know there was an incoming message. He reached for the handset, dropped the earpiece into place and felt his gut tighten instinctively. This late in the game the pilot was too seasoned to think even for a moment that it was going to be good news.

"TORTURE ME," the Iraqi said fiercely. "Kill me if you want. You'll get nothing from me. I'll gladly go to meet God."

Calvin James glanced up from the dossier Phoenix had been faxed concerning their captive. He snapped off his penflash and left the small, cramped cellar dark.

Maimun sat tied in a chair in the center of the cellar. His face was pale from the pain of his wound. A sheen of perspiration covered his features, softening the hard lines the years had put there. His clothing was sweat-stained, and he smelled of the sewer where the team had bagged him.

The air inside the cellar was cloying, thanks to the odors of fruit, vegetables and wine. An unused electric light hung from the mud-brick ceiling. The only illumination came from an adjustable lantern sitting on the floor beside

McCarter. The lanky Briton was stretched out along the wall. He used a penknife to pare chunks from an apple, then ate them from the blade.

Katz stood against the opposite side of the cellar. A wicked hook hung at the end of his right arm. The soft light from the lantern made him look grim and sinister.

Looking at the harsh glint in his leader's eyes, James wasn't so sure he could have remained as vocal as Maimun concerning a willingness to receive pain or die. Katz looked only too willing to comply. The ex-SEAL put the dossier away and stood, ducking his head to keep it safely from the low ceiling. He wrapped his hand around the haft of the survival knife hanging from his combat harness, closed the distance between himself and Maimun and leaned down to feel the man's hot breath against his face. He maintained eye contact.

Maimun didn't blink.

James let the tension build. According to the terrorist's files that Kurtzman had forwarded, Maimun was a deadly adversary. The man had been responsible for more than a dozen assassinations and had coordinated at least three airport bombings over the past ten years.

"You buying into his tough-guy front he's projecting?" James asked without taking his eyes away.

McCarter paused in his attack on the apple, holding the bite at his lips while he smiled. "Oh, yeah, mate. I buy it. Man's too one-tracked to worry about his own arse."

James grinned evilly. "Not much of an ass left, anyway, after Manning got through digging the bullet out."

"You can't make me talk," Maimun roared. His voice died against the mud walls of the cellar. The room was a safehouse sometimes used by the CIA. Price had turned it up on her files and had given them the address. "I'll die before I tell you anything."

"You already had that chance," James said. "You blew it. Wimped out."

Maimun screamed with rage and jerked against the ropes that bound him to the chair. Realizing the futility of his struggle, he curled his lips back and prepared to spit.

James clapped a big hand over their prisoner's mouth, making the man choke on the spittle and turn away coughing. The ex-SEAL straightened and moved out of range.

"Man's a believer," McCarter said. He finished the apple and tossed the core into the plastic bag the team had ready to remove all signs of their presence when they left the cellar. "Going straight to heaven when he dies."

"We could make him earn it," James said. "Make him pay his dues before he goes." He studied their prisoner's face.

Only anger colored Maimun's cheeks. There was no sign of fear.

James sighed inwardly. Katz had been right. There was no dealing with the men they faced. Pain and fear of death couldn't open them up. Still, he'd had to try. Minutes counted for everything at this stage of the play. Too many innocents had already died from the madness spewing over the Gulf region.

There was a knock at the door, and James's hand drifted down to cover the butt of the Beretta holstered at his hip. A familiar cadence echoed through the thick wooden panels.

McCarter threw the bolts and stepped back to allow Encizo and Manning entrance to the cellar. The Cuban handed a small tan case to Katz. Without looking at it the Israeli tossed it to James, who caught it deftly. It was light and innocent in appearance.

"The embassy people?" Katz asked.

"No problems," Manning replied, "and no questions. Barb must have some kind of connection with those people."

Katz nodded. "Calvin?"

James opened the case and gazed at the hypodermic syringe and vial of clear liquid inside. "Give me a couple of minutes." He pulled on sanitary gloves, then inserted the needle into the vial and drew off some of its contents. He thumped the side of the hypodermic to get all the air out. "I'm going to need some help holding him down."

Stepping forward, McCarter kicked over the chair containing Maimun. The terrorist crashed to the earthern floor where he'd be even less of a threat. Manning and McCarter held the man with obvious effort. The big Canadian cursed when Maimun's teeth found his leg.

Leaning down, James ripped away the man's uniform sleeve and slipped the hypodermic home. He hit the plunger and released the scopolamine into Maimun's system.

Arabic curses filled the cellar as James, Manning and McCarter drew back.

After disposing of the hypo, James hunkered down in front of Maimun. "Go ahead and fight it, guy. Flailing around like this is only going to make it work faster."

The terrorist's gaze was already turning glassy. His struggles slowed.

"Calvin?" Katz asked.

James motioned to Manning. Together they righted the chair and their prisoner. "He's all yours, Yakov."

Approaching, Katz said, "Then let's find out what he does know."

STRUGGLING TO KEEP from flinching, Barbara Price stood beside Aaron Kurtzman's desk and watched the news footage replay on the big wall screen at the end of the room.

Kurtzman watched in tight-lipped silence, his fist clenched around the tennis ball he used to work off tension when he was feeling too much stress.

Price wanted to look away as the terrorist stepped out into view of the news camera. The man was clad in bulky garments, his face masked by a hooded visor. A hose with a smoking tongue of yellow flame curling from it rested in his gloved hands. Without warning the man shouldered the hose like a rifle and turned slightly to reveal the oblong cylinders strapped across his back. An orange-and-black ball of flame mushroomed from the hose and enveloped a half-dozen men sleeping in the alley. Some of them died instantly. Two of them weren't so fortunate. They rose up in jerking leaps, like two flaming stick-specters. Sparks jumped from their arms and legs as they tried to run. Fiery footsteps followed them out into the street. One of them was hit by a passing car, plastering the flaming corpse across the windshield. The other dropped short of the sidewalk and lay burning.

Instinctively Price's hand dropped to the frequency control and she dialed in the Washington, D.C., police department. According to the dialogue she found there, patrol cars were already en route and the SWAT teams were a heartbeat behind.

"Where's Able?" she asked.

On-screen the bulky figure lumbered on, pursued at a discreet distance by the television camera. Other sudden blazes let her know the terrorist with the flamethrower wasn't alone. The news team had been spared so that they could broadcast the terrorists' message to the United States. From the comments coming from the television audibles, the reporters were in shock, following the line of carnage through Washington's homeless section unconsciously. The reporter and cameraman sounded young, naive. Price knew they'd be neither after tonight.

"Their plane left Dulles almost twenty minutes ago," Kurtzman answered. "Do you want me to call them back?"

"No." Price forced herself to breathe, forced her hands to unclench so that she could work the desk controls. "No. It'll be over before they can get back." She punched a button, banished the replay and caught up with the real-time loop in the broadcast again.

On-screen the camera switched points of reference as the first of the Washington police cars roared onto the scene. One of the terrorists unleashed a long blast from his flame-thrower, scattering flames thirty feet long that intercepted the car and spread fire across its hood. It caught immediately. The two patrolmen inside abandoned the vehicle at once. Their handguns brought the terrorist down an instant before one of the officers went up like a stack of kindling.

Price watched, mesmerized, unwilling to believe the horror she saw before her. But she knew it was real. She could hear the screams of the dying coming at her. The other computer operators in Kurtzman's workroom had stopped what they were doing to watch the events unfolding on the screen.

Gunfire punctuated the voices of the men and the shrill of traffic noises. Abruptly the video and audio transmissions ended when a big cop in Washington PD colors dropped over the reporter and cameraman team. Something broke, then even the whisper of voices left the room.

Price swept the headset away, feeling her knees tremble slightly as her imagination reenacted the horror she'd just witnessed.

"Jesus," Kurtzman breathed.

"Barbara."

Price shifted her attention to Carmen Delahunt. "Yes?"

"Carl Lyons is on line four. He's asking about the attack we just saw on television."

Scooping up the headset, Price held it to the side of her face. "Carl?"

"I'm here, Barb. We just heard about it. We were wondering what we could do."

"Nothing," she replied, then softened her voice. "You people have your assignment down in Florida, Carl. At best all you'd be able to do here is help defend a holding position. And holding positions aren't going to save lives. We need to turn this thing around and take an aggressive role while we still have the chance. It's your responsibility to try to turn up that chance in Miami."

"Understood. You people take care of yourselves till we make it back."

"You do the same." Price broke the connection.

Kurtzman looked up, radio headgear held to one ear. "Police snipers have put down the guys carrying flame throwers."

"What about losses?"

"It's unconfirmed. I've heard three police officers are down. Maybe as many as fourteen civilians are dead."

A phone rang. Price glanced down and saw that it was Brognola's private line. "Carmen?"

"Yes?"

"Get a lab team assigned to that area. We'll worry about the liaisons for the PD later."

"Right."

Lifting the receiver, Price said, "Hello."

"Are you aware of the situation down in the metro area?" Brognola asked without preamble.

"We're working on it now."

"Able Team?"

"No. They're out of the picture."

"Where?"

"Miami."

"What's going on there?"

"A presidential debate featuring Senator Cates Murray."

"The leading contender for the Democrats?"

"Right. Aaron broke more of the New York files. Murray's one of the terrorists' top targets."

"Has Murray been warned?"

"I had him contacted through the Justice Department."

"But he's not moving."

"No. I guess he figures the publicity will help him in the presidential race."

"If he lives so long," Brognola said.

Price watched the wall screen at the end of the room shift perspectives. A British television link swept them away to an area north of Baghdad, revealing a failed attack made by a group of Kurds on horseback. Dead men and horses lay sprawled across the ground beneath the late-evening sun. "How's Leo?"

"He's stable," Brognola said. "I'm still at the hospital with him. Angelina and the kids are here."

"Under guard?"

"I brought a small platoon of federal marshals with me. Nobody's going in or out of his room, or around his family without the proper paper."

"How bad is it?"

"He'll mend. The docs said the bullets penetrated his chest and collapsed a lung, but he'll be up and around just like new in a few weeks."

Price noted that Brognola's voice didn't carry the enthusiasm he was trying to muster. The wall screen had moved on to Kuwait City, but she found nothing new there.

"Have you relinked with Phoenix Force?" Brognola asked.

"Less than thirty minutes ago." Price checked her watch and found that her guess was accurate. "They cracked Maimun and are proceeding toward the terrorist base in Jerusalem. It's still touch and go there with the Israeli military and the Mossad."

"And Striker?"

"I've got Jack on the horn," Kurtzman said. "He's only minutes away from the pickup zone."

"I still don't like the idea of a Baghdad insertion at this stage of the operation," Price said. "Especially with the Russian wild cards in the deck."

"Nobody does," Brognola growled, "but it's the only hand we've got to play at this point."

"I know," Price said grimly.

9

Gripping his end of the body bag tightly, the Executioner trotted through the maelstrom of whirling sand toward Grimaldi's waiting Huey. The rest of the mercenary unit followed close behind, already divided up into three groups. He helped set the corpse inside the bay, then strapped it in place. A fine layer of dust already clung to the black material.

Four radio headsets dangled from the top of the helicopter's bay area. He slid into one, keyed it to life, then took up a position by the door as the rest of the group clambered into the Huey. Another body bag joined the first, then seven men spread out across the helicopter.

"Nighthawk Leader," Bolan called softly.

"Go."

The desert sand around the three helicopters was barren except for small dust puffs that jetted silver in the waning moonlight. Daybreak was only minutes away.

"We're aboard."

"Check." Grimaldi's voice continued on, firm and strong as he checked with the other two pilots. Everything cleared, the pilot gave the order to lift.

Through the bay doors Bolan saw the desert fall away when the skids lifted free of the sand. The Iraqi outpost was still wreathed in scattered flames. Bodies lay prone over sandbag walls and behind dunes. Black splotches that had been burned onto the desert floor by explosives stood stark against the light color of the sand. Nothing alive was left down there.

"Striker?"

Bolan keyed the mike onto the intercom frequency. "Yeah, Jack."

"I got Stony Base on the line with a request to put you through ASAP."

"On my way." Bolan disengaged from the headset and left it dangling again. Shouldering his M-16, he swung around the bay outside the helicopter, felt the wind tug at him for a moment, then opened the passenger side door and moved into the cockpit proper.

Grimaldi looked tired and needed a shave, but his hand was steady on the stick.

Accepting the headgear the pilot handed over, Bolan dropped into the empty seat and belted up. His eyes scanned the radar quickly. The screen was empty, but with the nap-of-the-earth type flying the Hueys were doing, nothing would register until they were on top of it. Ready lights glowed on the armament systems.

The warrior keyed the mike and listened to the scrambler kick to life in the frequency. "Stony Base, this is Stony One. Over."

"Roger, Stony One. You've reached Stony Base." Barbara Price's voice was clear and firm. "New intel has just come in concerning Iraqi interests. I'm patching you through to Watchdog now. Stony Base standing by."

The pitch whistled shrilly, then Brognola's voice filled the void left by white noise. "Stony One, this is Watchdog. Over."

"Go, Watchdog. You have Stony One. Over."

"Your instincts regarding possible Russian influence have been confirmed," Brognola said. "The Man has admitted their involvement puts a new spin on the current situation. Over."

"Agreed. Over."

"We also now know that Shawiyya is no longer fronting Iraqi interests. He's been replaced behind the scenes by Hamoud Jaluwi. Over."

"You've got confirmation on that? Over."

Grimaldi pulled a scarred metal thermos from beside his seat and handed it over. Bolan unscrewed the top and poured half a cup of coffee.

"Negative, Stony One," Brognola answered. "It's pure speculation at our end. But we did get the bastard's picture during Shawiyya's funeral services. He was with Semyon Zagladin. Ring any bells? Over."

"Russian KGB," Bolan replied. "Special projects leader for Directorate Thirteen. Over."

"That's the guy," Brognola responded without enthusiasm. "Once we made the connection, the Man put a call through to Moscow on the QT." The head Fed hesitated.

Bolan waited, fitting it together in his mind and knew the tentacled monster stemming from Baghdad had just sprouted another head like the mythical hydra. With some of the Middle Eastern countries hanging in the balance, undecided where to throw their loyalties, the presence of the Russian propaganda machine could make a lot of difference, perhaps even a world of difference. And the ongoing friendly overtures between Russia and the United States wouldn't be ignored by Israel. They could very easily be persuaded to see American involvement in the current crisis as a threatening posture. And once they did, the Executioner was grimly aware that total war was only a stone's throw away.

"It was a neat setup," Brognola went on. "An American agent was framed for the death of Jaluwi during an impassioned speech against the United States and Israel. Then Jaluwi and the KGB took Shawiyya down, knowing everyone would think the U.S. was behind it."

Bolan broke into the lapse in communication. "So where do I fit in? Over."

"The Russians have agreed to a meet in Baghdad. The Man wants you to handle it. Over."

"I'm not exactly ambassadorial material," the Executioner said. "And, at this point, I don't want to be part of a deal that's going to strand these people and leave them at the mercy of the Iraqis. Over."

"Understood, Stony One. The Man feels the same way. We're there to do a job. We're not pulling out till it's done. That's why he wants you to head up the meet. He figures if you deliver the message in person, they'll receive it undiluted and in the spirit in which it was intended. Over."

"Affirmative, Watchdog. When is the meet scheduled? Over."

"At 1900 hours your time. We've got no umbrella on this one. We're either there or they rule it a no-show. Over."

Bolan took out his map case, found a street map of Baghdad and spread it across his knees. He finished the coffee and screwed the cup back on the thermos. "Where's the meet? Over."

Brognola reeled off the address.

Marking the location indelibly in his mind after finding it with a forefinger, Bolan folded the map and put it away. "I'll want in as early as possible to do a recon of the area. Over."

"Agreed. Over."

"It'll mean breaking off the present retreat," Bolan said. "Once the Iraqi and Russian intel machines start rolling through this area, penetration of Baghdad will be even harder. If I'm going to go, now's the time. Over."

The head Fed agreed. "We've got you a calling card scheduled." In terse sentences he explained about the bombing raid the President had authorized against Baghdad. "Provided you and the Russians make the meet on time, the bombing run will take place within minutes. The Man figures it'll give weight to your words that we're committed to this thing. But you'll have to watch your ass. Over."

"Affirmative. With me gone, though, we need to get an intel package out to Eldridge and Desert Lightning. Bring him up to speed on the overall picture without going into too many of the particulars so he can be prepared to take care of the unit. Over."

"Acknowledged," Brognola said. "Stony Base? Over."

"Give me five minutes," Price replied, "and eyes-only paper will hit Eldridge's desk. Over."

Bolan nodded. Price had already been a step ahead of him in his thinking, reminding him that the lady knew her business. "Fair enough, Stony Base. Anything else, Watchdog? Over."

"Nothing here, big guy. Just update me after the meet. Over."

"That's affirmative," Bolan said. "Over."

"Stay hard, Stony One. Watchdog out."

The secondary connection rippled out of the com/net.

"What's the situation there, Stony Base? Over."

"We don't have time to go into everything, Stony One. Suffice for the moment to say that things could be worse. We're still taking losses all the way around. You'll get a full debrief as soon as you're on friendly ground again. Over."

"Roger, Stony Base. Stony One out."

Price cleared the frequency.

Hanging up the headset, Bolan knew things had gone bad for the Stony Man mission if Price didn't want to talk to him about it. She'd put him in his place tactfully. She was mission controller. All he needed to know at the moment was what obstacles lay before him and his present goal. Soldiers died more quickly when they tried managing more than one

battlefield at a time. She knew he had his hands full with
Kuwait and the tentacles leading from Iraq.

He turned his thoughts to the Baghdad meet. Zagladin
was a dangerous adversary, one who wouldn't hesitate to put
a knife between the shoulder blades of a friend to accom-
plish his mission. The big warrior had the feeling Khalid
Shawiyya had learned that point a little late in his relationship with the Russians.

Hamoud Jaluwi was a wild card. The Syrian had already
proved himself as a crafty and willing enemy. Bolan was sure
there were more surprises ahead.

"Find a place we can set down, Jack," Bolan said.
"There's been a few changes in the play."

FORCING HERSELF to put aside the confusing emotions that
swirled inside her, Talia Alireza dropped the short distance
from the bay of the helicopter to the ground. Her booted
feet sank at once into the loose sand. The rotors still buzzed
overhead, and she fitted her scarf over her lower face to keep
the dust out.

She walked past the middle Huey, kept herself from staring at the body bag that contained Jimoh and found the big
American ordering the mercenaries to carry the corpses out
of the lead chopper.

Anger flared in her at once. The mission had been more
costly than she'd have believed. Now this added confusion.
"What the hell's going on?" she demanded.

Bolan turned to look at her, his own scarf hanging at his
neck, leaving his lower face free of the dirt and grit that
filmed his cheeks and forehead. "Change in plans," he said
simply. "I've got to have this helicopter."

"Why?"

"Privileged information, soldier."

She ignored the veiled warning that should have sheathed
her claws. Her grip on the professionalism that had guided

her through her career as a mercenary slipped. "Haven't enough of my people died for you tonight?"

His gaze was cool, neutral.

Taking a step closer, putting him within reach and invading his personal space, she gave vent to the unexplainable anger that roiled inside her. "By doubling up on the other two helicopters, you're putting the rest of my team at risk."

"Can't be helped," he said in a soft voice. "We've got new intel on a situation that won't wait."

"With the extra weight on board," Alireza went on, "we might not make it back to Kuwait City."

"You have options."

"What?" She put her face only inches from his, looking up at him now, her fists clenched at her sides.

He didn't back away at all.

"You mean we can throw out the bodies of our dead."

"That's one option."

The calm in his voice only set off her anger more. "Your people hired our skills, paid us to take chances with our lives, mister, but you didn't buy our souls. We're leaving no one here."

"Your choice, Commander." He turned away and headed back toward the lead Huey.

The past crowded in on Alireza, filled her head with visions of the little girl with no past, no parents, no people and no future. Images of Jimoh and the others streamed through there, as well. Unable to stop herself she went after Bolan, laid a hand on his shoulder, then threw the weight of her whole body into a palm-heel strike as he turned. The blow caught the American in the face, not in the nose as she'd intended because he was quicker than she'd thought, but on the cheek.

Tension ran through the group of men ringing them. She was dimly aware of the low conversation that started within the ranks.

The Executioner's head was rocked back by the blow, and he sank back into a defensive crouch. Never once did he try to hit her. Some of the mercenaries already brandished handguns. The American pilot's 9 mm pistol was locked in his fist, but he looked uncertain as to what to do next.

A trickle of blood leaked down to Bolan's chin from a split lip. Keeping his eyes on her, he wiped it away with the back of his hand. "Anything else you'd care to add?" he asked in a voice that held no challenge or anger.

Sudden violence between the two groups was balanced on the edge of a razor blade, and Alireza knew it. And the big American's calm was the only thing keeping it from going past the point of no return.

She released a pent-up breath and stared into the ice-blue depths of the warrior's eyes. "I'm not going to be kept in the dark. My people aren't going to go any farther or take any more chances on just your say-so. I stopped being just a pawn in espionage games a long time ago. Either tell me what's going on or you and your friend have a long walk back in the desert."

He nodded. "Fine. Let's take a walk." Turning away, he started without her, telling the pilot, "Jack, stay here. Keep it loose."

The pilot nodded.

Alireza lengthened her stride and caught up to the man, walking abreast of him. For a hundred yards the silence remained between them. From her peripheral vision she was aware of Ben Fenwick, one of the Britons in her employ, dropping into a sniping position atop one of the nearby dunes.

Striker took in Fenwick, as well, but ignored the threat. In terse sentences he outlined the proposed meet between himself and the KGB liaison in Baghdad.

The anger washed away as he spoke. A certainty crystalized within her by the time he finished. She knew she surprised them both when she said, "I'm going with you."

He started to protest. She could tell by his body language.

She ticked off points on her fingers. "You don't know the language. You don't know the city. Your helicopter pilot can't be an escape route and your backup at the same time. You haven't had, and don't have, time to make any preparations. And you'd be an idiot not to think this was some kind of setup to take you out of the action." She paused. "I'm out of fingers on this hand, but I could go on."

He was quiet for a moment, then said, "Fine," and started back toward the waiting helicopters.

Alireza stood there in amazement, then collected herself and followed. She wasn't sure of the forces that drove her, only knew that she had to make the trip with him to see what was waiting there.

But, even though she'd be ready for it, she told herself she'd be surprised if the American didn't try to throw her from the helicopter after they'd gotten under way.

"THE MARK OF THE BEAST."

Lieutenant Colonel Joshua Eldridge heard Paul's voice as he stared at the top-secret file spread across his desktop. The enlarged picture of Hamoud Jaluwi held him in thrall. He brushed a big thumb over the new scar marring the Syrian political leader's forehead.

"The mark of the Beast," the whisper came again.

And Eldridge knew it was so. For a time he'd believed the mark to be worn by Gorbachev, but there were no longer uncertainties here. He knew he was staring at the Antichrist.

A chill filled him, leaving his lungs constricted.

He made himself move and stuffed the papers back inside the pouch his communications people had placed them in after receiving them. He ignored the cup of coffee that had grown cold at his elbow, left his tent and stepped outside.

He breathed in the cold desert air, terrified by what he knew to be true now. The stars seemed so cold and so far away. He had to clench his teeth to keep them from chattering. Rather than stand there freezing as he tried to come to grips with the new knowledge that fired him, he took up a circuit of Desert Lightning's temporary base.

A sentry saluted Eldridge as he passed. Eldridge returned the salute automatically. He crossed behind the motor pool, heard the low strains of a radio and decided not to do anything about it at the moment. If it was still there on his way back, he'd mention it to the duty officer.

His thoughts whirled inside his mind. The espionage people responsible for uncovering the KGB plot and the faked assassination of Jaluwi were under the mistaken impression that they knew what was going on. They thought the Middle Eastern crisis had been kicked off by terrorist and Soviet machinations. They had no idea what the truth really was.

On the outskirts of the camp's perimeter now, Eldridge slipped a penflash from his pocket and started to examine the camou cover over one of the tanks. The light fell from his fingers, the yellow beam throwing a crooked ellipse over the desert sand.

He knelt, started to reach for it, then heard a banshee wail that froze him. Grabbing for his service automatic, he gazed around the base camp, surprised that no one else appeared to have heard the sound.

"Joshua."

Swiveling his head, Eldridge looked toward the sound of Paul's voice. Amazement coursed through him when he looked back. Where the fallen penflash had been, a bush now stood, burning with unearthly flames that didn't consume it.

Before he could think about the possibilities, Eldridge stretched out a hand and felt the incredible heat that seemed about to blister his skin.

"No, Joshua," Paul's voice called softly. "Don't come any closer."

Eldridge withdrew his hand.

"Take off your boots," Paul said, "because this place is holy ground."

With trembling hands Eldridge did as he was told. He tossed his boots to one side, followed with his socks and remained on his knees before the flaming bush.

"Know that I am from the God of your father, the God of Abraham, the God of Isaac and the God of Jacob," Paul's voice went on. "Are there any doubts in your heart, Joshua?"

Eldridge's voice was a croak. "None."

"I know, my friend, and He knows, as well. Now is the time come for all to be revealed to you, and for your part to be made known to you concerning His plans. You've seen the face of the one bearing the mark of the Beast."

"Yes."

"It's the time of Armageddon, Joshua," Paul said, "and God has chosen you to be His instrument."

"What am I supposed to do?"

"The world has died once by water. This time it shall perish by fire, and that fire shall be set by your hand."

"How?"

"You know the method, Joshua, all you need to know is the time. The children of Israel house nuclear weapons within their homeland. It's within your ability to get those weapons. Do this now and raise an army that will fight for the will of God."

"Where do I find this army?"

"They are here. Around you. You'll know them when you see them. Some will stay with you until the end. Others will know fear and turn from you as Peter turned from Christ."

"After I get the nuclear weapons, what then?" Eldridge didn't have any doubts about his ability to get his hands on them. No one could stand against the force that drove him. He glanced at his hands and saw the same fiery glow surrounding the burning bush suffusing his own flesh.

"All will be made clear to you in the time that it's needed," Paul said. "Just accept what is put before you. Accept the fact that God has chosen you to deliver the world from the evils and perversities that have become unconquerable blights on it. Take your army and drive toward Babylon, where God has once before shown men the folly of their ways."

Eldridge bowed his head.

"Now arise. I have one last gift to give you."

Standing, Eldridge watched in amazement as Paul rose up from the smoke of the burning bush. The flames flickered through the man's flesh, making him appear translucent.

"Step forward," Paul said, moving forward, as well.

Acid seemed to boil through Eldridge's veins for a moment as the apparition dissolved and was sucked in through the pores of his skin. Then the pain passed and only calm filled him.

When Paul's voice spoke again, it came from inside his head. "Know this, Joshua. No longer will you see or hear me. I leave you with God's work, and it's His voice you'll hear as you do His will. I'll see you again on the other side."

A tranquility like none Eldridge had ever experienced hummed within him. He stared at the burning bush, filled with the sense of purpose that was rooted to his very soul.

Someone called his name behind his back. Eldridge turned and saw the chaplain standing there.

"Sir?" the chaplain said with obvious hesitation.

"What do you want?"

The chaplain stuck his hands into his pockets, still not sure how to act. "The men asked me to perform a church service later today, seeing that there might not be time after that. I was wondering if you'd be interested in joining us, perhaps say a few words to them."

Looking back where the burning bush had been, Eldridge saw only the penflash lying there. He smiled to himself, then reached down for it, turned it off and pocketed it. Without missing a beat he reached down for his boots and socks. "I'll be right there. I wouldn't miss it for the world."

MACK BOLAN HAD SURPRISED himself by not attempting to throw Talia Alireza from the helicopter the first time the chance had presented itself. Maybe his decision had surprised her, too, because she'd remained inordinately quiet during the two-hour flight into Iraq. They'd rested, eaten soup from a thermos and napped briefly while Jack Grimaldi had jockeyed the Huey transport chopper through Iraqi air and ground defenses using Stony Man Farm's access to Star Wars telemetries. There had only been one close call when they had to go to ground and use camou netting to conceal themselves from a fighter jet patrol. The satellite systems kept an accurate eye on the air lanes through Iraq.

Now, four hours later with the desert sun burning down on him and feeling—at best—only as worn down as he had before taking the sudden jaunt into Iraq, the warrior was glad of the woman's company. Whatever inner turmoil had pushed her over the edge earlier that morning gave no evidence of being in Alireza now. She was confident, competent and skilled in the desert.

But he still counted her as a potential loose cannon when the chips were down. And that was the reason that, although he'd told her about the meet, he hadn't mentioned the planned American bombing run. If they became separated, she wouldn't be able to give away the knowledge if she was captured.

Even though he'd agreed to let her come with him, he'd already decided to cut his losses if she became unhinged again. She didn't know where Grimaldi would be waiting with the helicopter. Maybe she'd noticed they'd been using doublespeak when they set up the coordinates, and maybe she hadn't.

Heat soaked through Bolan's combat boots as he walked. Sand had already found its way inside the tough leather, but he'd given up any hope of finding a way to keep it out. Occasional stops were made to empty it out when it became too uncomfortable to go on.

Dressed in a burnoose and headpiece, the warrior still felt as if he was sweltering. But he knew he wouldn't have lasted unprotected from the merciless desert sun.

He squinted, aware that his depth perception had been fouled by the rolling rise of the heat waves around them. Black smoke curled up from the curve of the desert in the foreground. The color denoted petroleum products. Wood smoke would have burned white or gray.

He glanced at Alireza and saw her nod to let him know she'd seen it, too. In the open desert as they were, there was no place to take cover.

Beneath the burnoose he wore the Desert Eagle .44 on his hip, the Beretta 93-R in customary shoulder leather and a MAC-10 strapped in a Whipit sling under his right arm. His combat harness carried additional magazines for his weapons, and other combustibles, but he wasn't equipped for an extended confrontation with Iraqi troops.

He snapped on his ear-throat headset, quickly running through the frequencies. There was no chatter on any of the channels. It was a good sign, unless there was an Iraqi unit on the other side of the hill maintaining radio silence.

Alireza closed the distance between them.

"What do you think?" he asked.

She pointed.

He followed the line of her finger and saw the lone vulture circling overhead, a speck in the distance but still possessing the familiar predatory circling movement now that he'd noticed it.

Long minutes later they made the top of the hill.

Bolan's stomach clenched at the sight of the carnage spread out before them. From the bits and pieces of radio reports he'd managed to listen to during the flight, he already knew about the Iraqi attacks against the Kurds.

"Oh, my God," the woman said softly, then started down the hill.

Bolan followed, his hand on the Desert Eagle through the slits he'd made in the burnoose.

Tank tracks had chewed through the baked surface of the desert, turning up hills and jagged ridges that had redefined the terrain. The black smoke coiled from the burned-out husk of a T-55. The tribe hadn't gone down without marking their enemy.

But the blood price demanded in return had been incredible. Bodies of men and horses were scattered across the narrow mouth of a box canyon that butted up against the incline. Figures moved within the death ground. When he got closer, he saw they were women and children. Even the eldest boys among them hadn't seen a dozen years yet.

The Kurds turned at their approach, some of the women raising rifles and swords uncertainly.

Less than forty feet out Alireza said, "Stay here," then dropped her cowl to reveal her veiled face so the women would know she was female, as well. She walked forward, her empty hands held at shoulder level, speaking in what sounded to be an Arabic dialect.

Bolan stood with his hand on the .44, scanned the broken ridges of the canyon around them and tried to figure out how long ago the battle with the Iraqis might have taken place, how close the enemy might still be.

As he watched, Alireza walked into the group of women and children. Dozens of voices pursued her, racked with pained emotions. Bolan could understand the feelings even though he didn't know the words. He'd learned Vietnamese through the same introduction, learned the words for grief, loss and terror first, then learned how to ask for food.

Long minutes passed as Alireza stayed mired in the conversations. Finally a young girl separated from the group and ran quickly through the destroyed camp to round up two horses. She came back, handed their reins to Alireza, then backed away.

With a final few words the mercenary turned from the women and led the horses to Bolan. "Don't say anything and just mount up," she instructed. "So far they haven't noticed that you're American. I told them that you were my husband, that you were mute."

Without a word Bolan pulled himself up into the saddle. Although foam still flecked the horse, it felt strong. The woman kicked her horse and took the lead, heading toward Baghdad.

By Bolan's estimation the city lay less than ten miles away. Once the Kurd camp was behind them, he nudged his horse and trotted up alongside the mercenary commander.

Her face was hard-set, resolute. "They were attacked by the Republican Guard. Their husbands and fathers were slaughtered down to the last man. The soldiers tried to attack them, as well, but they held them until their commanders gave up and retreated."

Bolan remained silent. There was nothing he could say. More vultures had joined the first in the crisp blue sky.

"This land is filled with a madness," Alireza said. She looked at him, demanding, "Can't you feel it?"

"It's war," he replied. "War doesn't make sense unless you believe in it. It's a system within itself. Historians add labels to wars later when they think they have a perspective on all the events. Doesn't mean you have to buy into that label."

"I've seen wars before. I've fought in them. But this . . . this reaches beyond anything I've ever known."

"Maybe you've never let yourself get this close to a situation."

She shook her head vehemently. "No. I'm not close to this country. I spent a long, forgotten childhood here that was filled with deceit and unhappiness. That's all."

Bolan studied the skylines, thinking for a moment that he could see the golden towers of Baghdad in the distance.

"Why are you involved here?" she asked after a moment. "Did you feel the call to war like so many of your American compatriots said they did?"

He looked at her and answered honestly. "You mean, was this a response to threatened national pride?" He shook his head. "I came here to do a job, and that job is taking out the people behind the terrorist action killing allied soldiers in Kuwait and civilians in the United States."

"There are innocents and civilians in this country, too."

"If the madmen engineering this are put down," the Executioner said, "the suffering of the innocents will end here, too."

"You're wrong," she said softly. "No one represents the people who live here. The American government is just as guilty as the Iraqis and Russians for what is threatening to consume this country. If they didn't involve themselves in matters of state in the Middle East, there'd be no one to fight."

"The Iranians and Iraqis had a war not so long ago themselves."

"That was aided and abetted by American interference."

"Depends on your point of view," Bolan said. "The Middle East has a long history of warring cultures, all the way back to biblical times. Accepting this place as the origin of civilization, you could say that war was taught here, then was spread out and given to the rest of the world. Think of it as a wound. It festers first on the inside, then affects the rest of the organism. A wound heals from the outside to the inside, then becomes complete again. In order to heal itself maybe the Middle East needs outside interference."

"There's no way to rationalize this."

"No, the problem is there's too many ways to rationalize what's happening over here. Politicians, businessman and religious leaders all have views on what's ultimately happening in the Middle East."

"And you?" she asked. "What do you believe?"

"That I can do some good here, can effectively spare some of the innocents that would otherwise be buried in this conflict."

"What if you're wrong?"

"I can't let myself believe that I am," Bolan answered truthfully.

Her expression showed that her curiosity wasn't satisfied. She kicked her heels into her horse and took the lead again as they started up another incline.

Bolan trailed her, letting her have her privacy because he needed some for thinking of his own. His gut told him Jaluwi, the Russians and the American bombing weren't the only dangers he might be facing in the coming hours.

10

The church service for the men of the Desert Lightning unit was held outdoors. A gentle wind blew in from the east, not enough to lift and twist the sand as it usually did, but it brought with it a cooling balm that was almost sensual when it touched Eldridge's skin.

Chaplain Harvey Prescott conducted his sermon from the open back of a two-and-a-half-ton truck. The American flag flew from the right side of the vehicle. Prescott stood behind a podium that had been quickly cobbled together from packing crates. Occasionally the public-address system would give out an electronic squelch or crackle.

Standing down and to the right of the truck, holding his hat in his clasped hands behind his back, Eldridge surveyed the crowd. Most of the Desert Lightning unit was there. Nearly all of them sat in ranked tiers along the sandy inclines of the bowl-shaped depression that held the encampment. Others sat in or near cav units they'd been working on. All of them had access to the service through the limited-range radio frequency that had been assigned for the service.

Eldridge ran a practiced eye over his troops. They were hard, lean fighting men. He was proud of every one of them, but wary, as well. Not all of them would make the cut into the army he'd been commanded to raise. But he knew he could find those who could follow the vision he was to deliver to them.

The chaplain's sermon had been bland, more perfunctory than inspired. Prescott finished with a brief prayer, then turned to Eldridge.

Without hesitation the colonel stepped up onto the truck bed and took the chaplain's place. Prescott got down and moved to the side of the vehicle.

Eldridge let his gaze sweep across the assembled soldiers, let the silence draw his listeners to him. Placing his hands on the podium, feeling the rough wood under his palms, he felt power he'd never known rise up inside him. His throat tightened with it, but there was no way to keep the feeling inside. Joy and reassurance thrilled through him. The Voice murmured inside his head and, though he couldn't hear the words, it calmed him, gave him confidence.

"I'm a fighting man by trade," he said loudly. His words tumbled and echoed over the sand dunes. "I've been taught to believe in the weapons I was given. Taught to believe in the training I've received. As fellow soldiers, you people are supposed to believe in the same things in times like these. Luck and belief in the Almighty are supposed to be something you don't count on." He paused. "But show me the man who hasn't found religion of one kind or another waiting in a fighting hole while bombs fell all around him. I know I have. Childhood prayers have come as easily to my lips as if those days were only yesterday."

An understanding chuckle passed through the crowd.

Eldridge raised a fist. "You know what I'm talking about. That call to religion and belief is never more strong in a man than when he's standing at the edge of battle, staring death in the eye. Since we began this campaign, you men have seen friends, associates and teammates die from the bullets and bombs of our enemies. We know it's not going to end with them."

The soldiers turned uneasy and solemn.

"But there's a force out there. One that can be your refuge and fortress as you go into battle. One that you can trust. And it'll deliver you from anything the Iraqis choose to throw at you. That truth can be your shield and buckler. Your fellows might die all around you, but you'll prevail. There's a higher reward for us than our enemies will ever know." He paused. "Believe...and you will know that reward for yourselves. Listen for the voice that will guide you and keep you safe. Open your hearts and let it in if you've always denied it before."

Their eyes were on him, attentions riveted.

"Our enemies have gathered themselves together against the souls of the righteous in this war, and they've spilled innocent blood. But if you listen to your hearts, use the courage that you can find in that force, we can be the instruments of a terrible and lasting vengeance against the Iraqis. That's my prayer." He paused. "And God keep each and every one of you under his watchful eye. Amen."

Slowly at first, then with increasing speed, the soldiers got to their feet. Individuals who hadn't taken off their hats before did so now. A thunderous well of applause rose around Eldridge as he stepped away from the podium.

The colonel glanced at Prescott and saw the surprise and shock etched on the man's face. Ignoring it, Eldridge walked through the mass of men that closed in around him. He gloried in the attention but didn't let the feeling show on his face. If he was going to take control of the situation and push it in the direction the Voice commanded, he had to show strength as well as conviction. He shook hands as he moved through the crowd, taking in the yells of support.

Once he reached his tent and the last vestiges of the crowd peeled away from him, he felt the trembling set in. The Voice spoke to him, building up his strength again. He closed his eyes and sat at his desk, resting his forehead on his knuckled hands. Perspiration, not all of it caused from the desert heat, covered his face.

"Permission to enter, Colonel," a voice called out.

Eldridge looked up and said, "Permission granted."

The man entered the tent and stood at ramrod attention, his hat tucked securely under his arm. "Sergeant McGrath reporting as requested, sir."

"At ease, gunney."

"Yes, sir." The man slumped into parade rest, his eyes resting on an invisible line six inches above Eldridge's head. "Permission to speak freely, sir?"

"Granted."

"That was a hell of a speech out there, sir. The men needed something like that. Having an officer take the lead in addressing the religious needs of his soldiers means a hell of a lot to them."

"Thank you, gunney." The Voice sounded in Eldridge's head, congratulating him on his success, promising more to come. The colonel leaned back in the folding chair. "Your words mean a lot to me."

The sergeant nodded.

Eldridge tapped the file in front of him with a forefinger. "You're familiar with Operation Toyworx?"

"Yes, sir. It's an American operation designed to liberate known nuclear weapons from the Israelis in the event the situation with Iraq appears imminently ballistic."

"And you're one of the tactical group leaders?"

"Yes, sir. There are three other tactical officers in Kuwait. Six more waiting stateside, plus—"

"The British forces have their own people ready to move in, as well."

"Yes, sir."

Eldridge stood, clasped his hands behind his back and walked around to the front of the desk. The sergeant remained eyes forward, staring at the wall behind the desk. "Do you believe in the politics behind this operation?"

"Yes, sir. Containment of hostile activity in the Middle East is our optimum objective. Even if it means ultimately alienating the Israelis. If they go off half-cocked, as they've given every indication of doing, the cost over here in American lives and the loss of American oil reserves could be astounding. There'd be nothing left to salvage."

"Yes." Eldridge nodded. "I'm activating your unit, Sergeant McGrath, under password ASKEW." He glanced at his watch. "Get your team together. You'll be leaving within the hour by way of a Chinook helicopter that's already been requisitioned and is en route from Kuwait City." Using Pollock's control codes, which had been in the file he'd received only hours ago, had cut out whatever questions might have been coming from the allied base in Kuwait City.

"What do we do with the recovered weapons?" McGrath asked.

"Proceed north," Eldridge said as he handed a folder across. "Your orders are in there. A special radio frequency has been established for your mission. You'll find the contact times and checkpoints listed. It'll be Operation Toyworx with a few wrinkles added. Your code name is Prometheus."

If McGrath recognized the name from Greek mythology as the firebringer, he gave no indication.

"Memorize the contents of that package," Eldridge said, "then destroy it."

"Yes, sir."

"Any questions?"

"No, sir."

"You're dismissed, Sergeant."

McGrath fired off a salute. "Thank you, sir. And God keep you."

"God keep you," Eldridge said automatically.

McGrath executed a sharp one-eighty turn and marched out the door.

"God keep you," Eldridge repeated, deciding he liked the way the phrase rolled from his lips. Crossing the room, he opened a metal thermos and poured himself a cup of lukewarm water. It tasted brackish, but he swallowed it, anyway. He couldn't afford to let his physical needs go unattended while he answered the spiritual ones.

Taking his hat from the desk, he put it on, then checked the action of his .45 and returned it to his hip holster. A pair of sunglasses from a drawer cut down on the desert glare when he stepped outside. He walked to his personal jeep, waved away the private who started out to act as his guard and keyed the engine to life.

Wheeling it around, he headed for the deuce-and-a-half where the church service had been held. Chaplain Prescott was finishing boxing the PA system when he got there.

"Harvey," Eldridge called as he killed the jeep and remained sitting behind the wheel.

"Colonel?" Uncertainty still shone in Prescott's eyes.

"Let me give you a lift back to your tent," Eldridge said. "That box is too damn heavy to be carrying it around in this heat."

"Yes, sir." Prescott stored the box on the rear deck of the jeep and took the passenger seat.

Firing up the jeep again, Eldridge steered toward the open desert behind the Desert Lightning encampment. He drove in silence for a moment before noticing Prescott fidgeting. "We'll get back your way in a moment. I want to take a look at the outer perimeters first."

"Yes, sir."

Cresting the dune, Eldridge rolled on through the shifting sea of sand and heat waves that lay before them. His hands trembled in anticipation of what he was about to do. Flexing them, he held the emotion in check.

"Sir," Prescott said, "I have a question."

"Ask."

"Are you feeling all right?"

Eldridge glanced at Prescott, not letting a smile touch his lips. "Never felt better in my life."

The chaplain appeared flustered. "I didn't mean to pry, sir, but after the episode in Kuwait City, and the speech earlier, I was concerned."

"I was just complimented concerning that speech," Eldridge said.

"Yes, sir. But it's kind of unusual for a commanding officer to take such an aggressive stand on religion in a military arm."

"We find ourselves in unusual times, soldier."

Prescott nodded. Hanging on to the seat as the jeep rode over the uneven terrain, he looked like a small, frightened man.

Twenty minutes passed.

"Sir," Prescott said, "we passed the outer camp perimeters some time ago."

"I know." Eldridge stopped the jeep by a clump of brush and small boulders. He clambered out of the vehicle. "Get out and stretch your legs for a moment before we head back."

Prescott got out, looking even more nervous.

Checking his watch again, Eldridge figured his return to the base would be approximately the same time as the arrival of the Chinook for Operation Toyworx. Security could be more concerned with keeping a low profile than in remembering who Eldridge came back with.

He faced Prescott and thought of the schism the man's continued presence could have caused within the Desert Lightning ranks. "What would you say, Chaplain, if I told you that the mission had changed?"

"I'd have to know more about the changes, sir."

"Suppose I informed you that God is now my CO and that He's set into play an operation whose objective is the birth of Armageddon and the Second Coming?"

Face blanching, Prescott didn't reply.

"You would stand in my way, Chaplain," Eldridge said softly. "I can see no other avenue for you to pursue. You'd bear false witness against me, make it impossible to carry out the work I've been assigned."

"You're crazy," Prescott said desperately. "You need help. We can get you help. Just relax and let me—"

Eldridge drew his .45. "You'd try to prevent me from doing God's work, Prescott. You'd try to bend His Word in your own interests." He squeezed the trigger.

The heavy-caliber bullet caught Prescott high in the chest and spilled him backward. Blood covered his black suit and stained the clerical collar.

Eldridge fired twice more, making certain of the kill. He let the smoking gun hang at the end of his arm while he looked down at the dead man. "There will be no false prophets in my army," he promised.

After taking the trenching tool from the back of the jeep, he said a prayer while he buried the corpse. He made the grave a shallow one because there were still many preparations to be made before the crusade could get under way.

TALIA ALIREZA SAT on her side of the empty building's underground parking garage and watched the big American.

Bolan sat cross-legged in the concrete dust and sand covering the cracked floor. A low-wattage lantern hung from the wall above his head. He worked with a pencil on the scale maps of the confrontation area he'd reproduced from memory and the street maps in his case.

Without warning the woman's stomach growled, sounding loud in the vaultlike quiet of the room.

"You should eat," Bolan said without looking up. His pencil brushed against the white paper, adding another dimension. "You need to keep your strength up. There's no way to tell what the next few hours will bring."

Ignoring the advice, Alireza returned her attention to her weapons. Even down here the dust seemed as determined as ever to creep in and foul the actions.

Bolan continued working in silence. The whisper of the pen across the paper was the only sound except for the noise the mercenary made while cleaning her M-16. As she watched him work, she knew patience wasn't a virtue with the big man. It was a well-learned skill necessary to survival.

Until now it was one she had always enjoyed, too. But she'd never considered it during a mission. It was something she'd taken for granted.

A light cramp trembled in her leg. Fatigue and stress had taken their toll on her body before the forced march into Baghdad. The horses had offered a physical challenge of another kind.

Finished with the rifle, she reached into her field pack and took out an MRE and two potassium tablets to combat the increasing leg cramps. She swallowed the tablets and ate quickly. Without a word Bolan joined her, his attention still consumed by the drawings he'd made.

There was no satisfaction from the meal, only a feeling of fullness that was almost uncomfortable. A glance at her watch showed it was only a few minutes after five. Nearly two hours remained before the meet.

She visualized the area again in her mind. Their present position was about ten blocks from the meeting place. The building they were in offered almost a dozen escape routes if they were discovered by roving patrols the Russian KGB agent might have employed. Getting out of the immediate terrain of the truce area would be dicey though, and she knew it. The American was taking a big chance by meeting with the Russians. Yet he hadn't seemed to hesitate about confronting them. Alireza suddenly realized she envied him his convictions.

"Have you always been so certain of what you were doing?" she asked when the man finished eating.

He set the empty MRE container to one side and pushed the paperwork he'd generated over for her consideration. "As you can see from the area, there aren't a lot of options to play with here. We can set the diversions around the inner perimeters, hope we aren't discovered while we're doing it, then hope we get lucky enough to get out safely if it turns sour."

She glanced at the papers. The drawings were startlingly accurate, showing craftsmanship, an artistic eye and a steady hand.

"You don't have to be part of this," Bolan told her. "I can take it from here."

She shook her head. "No. I'm going to be there. You'd be a fool not to want me in some kind of sniping position to cover a forced retreat."

"Yes, but you didn't sign on for this part of the operation."

She pointed to the paper. "This wasn't what I was talking about."

He regarded her silently.

Knowing he wasn't going to make it easy for her, she asked, "How do you know that your involvement here is right?"

"If it wasn't me, it would be someone else."

"But it *is* you. You're here because you want to be."

"Because I believe I can do the job."

"And because you believe that job is necessary?"

"Yeah, I believe it is."

"Some of the innocent people here are going to be hurt by your actions. Doesn't that bother you?"

He shifted and looked at her more intently. "Yes, it bothers me. It bothered me in Vietnam, and it bothered me in other places." Old hurts and painful memories gleamed in his blue eyes. "War is like that, Talia. It touches more than the combatants. Civilian casualties always run deep, too. I don't think of war as an answer. I think of it as a catalyst that makes people find new answers. But wars are fought to clear the rank and file so that new leaders can be found, a new peace negotiated. The war that was fought here last year wasn't finished. Too many of the old players were left in place. No new thinking emerged."

"The same can be said of your country."

"Perhaps. But I believe in my country, and in the visions the United States has always upheld. Freedom, the pursuit of happiness. There have been some who tried to corrupt those visions, but those ideals have always proved more lasting than those individuals. I haven't found anything—ever—that I'm more willing to believe in. And defend."

His words carried away into the silence cloaking the parking garage.

"Maybe that's the difference between us," she said. "You have a country to believe in, and I don't."

He hesitated, then the set of his body told her he'd decided to go ahead and speak what was on his mind despite whatever misgivings he had. "You can't look to another person for some answers, Talia. They have to come from within yourself. We all have needs at times that we don't understand, only know that they're there. We have to name them for ourselves, then either feed them or cut them out of ourselves."

"You're very eloquent when you choose to be," she said tightly.

"Only because the truth is eloquent when you know that's what you're hearing. I've served my time in the trenches. It's a place where you learn, or you die."

She nodded. "I've always thought of myself as so complete, so hard and so damn capable."

"You are."

"Thank you. But I've realized maybe I've been avoiding some questions I should have asked myself a long time ago."

He waited patiently for her to go on.

Instead she reached out and touched his face softly. Her fingers caressed his stubbled cheeks. Her lips found his. There was a need burning inside her, and she couldn't deny it any longer. She needed to give herself to something, something she believed in.

And there was the need she sensed between herself and this man. The physical attraction between them had been apparent to her from the start. Very few man had touched her so deeply, and it wasn't often that she'd been able to release her personal defenses so completely. But here in Baghdad there was only the two of them and a city of potential enemies.

Maybe the American felt the same way. She didn't know, couldn't know his mind. But his touch was gentle, uncertain until she made him know she knew what she wanted.

His arms slid around her more confidently, and she knew he was answering needs of his own. She helped him with their clothing, stoked the fire burning between them. The lantern reflected gleams from their sweating bodies. He used their clothing to make a pallet, then eased her down.

He covered her body with his, skin hot from more than just the stifled environment of the parking garage. He moved against her, pushed her over the edge of her release and kept her there. She let herself go, seized the rapture and clung as desperately to it as she did the man, kept the questions away from her mind and her soul, afraid of the answers that might come.

KATZ SPOKE SOFTLY as he looked over the city from the rooftop. *"Yerushalaim."*

McCarter glanced at him and cocked an eyebrow. An Uzi rested easily in the crook of his arm. Like his leader, the Briton wore black clothing and dark camou combat cosmetics to blend into the twilight descending over the city.

"A Hebrew word," Katz explained. "It's believed by many to be the source of Jerusalem's name. It means 'City of Peace.' "

"Well, mate, don't take it to heart. They misnamed Greenland, too."

Katz peered over the side of the three-story warehouse. The narrow street running behind the building was a spur off Herzl Boulevard. It straightened out here, then resumed its twisting approach to the Yad Vashem. Squinting, Katz could almost see the memorial in the distance. The thought of the memorial's impending destruction pained him greatly. The Yad Vashem represented the loss of the six million Jews who had died in the ovens and death camps of Adolf Hitler during World War II. Katz remembered the stories, the horrors that had been described to him while he was growing up. The Holocaust was a touchstone for the Jewish people, and something that was special to the Israelis.

Maimun's information under the effects of the scopolamine had been slow and disjointed. First they'd learned of the terrorist plan to destroy a Jewish monument. Katz had assumed the man was referring to the Wailing Wall, the most sacred of Jerusalem's landmarks to the Jews. He'd thought the terrorist cell was attempting the impossible. The Israeli army controlled most of the Old City now, and there was little chance the terrorists could penetrate the defenses the military had erected.

With continued questioning the real truth had come out and Phoenix Force had learned of the planned strike against the Yad Vashem.

Glancing back up, Katz saw an Israeli-made Huey skimming low over the Old City in the distance. The helicopter's searchlight trailed like a questing finger through the rise of uneven skyline. It was a grim reminder that—even if Phoenix was successful here—there was precious little margin for error.

"Katz."

Answering the thin hiss of Calvin James's voice in his ear, Katz thumbed the transmit button on his headset. "Go," he said softly.

"We've got a green light on the terrorist action. I'm looking at three—no, make that four—vehicles heading your way."

Katz adjusted the strap holding his Uzi across his midsection. Biting the cuff of the glove he wore on his left hand, he checked the tautness of the rappeling rope attached to his harness. Counting the Kevlar vest and his equipment, the line would have to support a lot of weight moving quickly to the ground three stories below. "Lay it out for us."

McCarter had already gone through the precheck before the jump and stood ready, out of sight, at the edge of the building.

"You've got a dark blue or black van in the lead," James said.

There was a hissing pop that Katz recognized as the air pistol James had been assigned for the beginning leg of the mission.

"It's marked," James went on.

"Do they know it?"

"Never heard a thing," James said. "With the air pressure reduced those paint pellets barely have the oomph to make the range. On top of the vehicles, firing from an angle, those pellets are rupturing like soap bubbles. Should get a nice spread pattern. Number two is a station wagon with blacked-out windows. Judging from the way it's riding, though, it's either got bad shocks or it's carrying a load."

Katz looked eastward, the sound of whining transmissions reaching him now.

"Number three's another van." The air pistol hissed again. "And number four's a Land Rover. They're all marked."

"What about Yusef Ijzim?"

"Haven't found him."

The terrorist leader's features were marked indelibly in Katz's mind. Kurtzman's files faxed from Stony Man after the interview with Maimun were very accurate. Ijzim had been photogenic, but he'd also been very slippery to deal with. The man had eluded law-enforcement agencies from a half-dozen European countries for almost twice as many years.

Katz intended the man's killing to be here, tonight. The Phoenix Force leader slid on his night vision goggles and stared down the alley. A field of overlapping greens lit up his vision, bringing the alley into sharp and strange relief.

"They're by me," James transmitted. "I'm on my way."

"Very good, Calvin," Katz said. "Gary?"

"Standing by."

"Rafael?"

"Awaiting your signal."

"Very good," Katz said. "Let's do this one by the numbers." He tested the slack in the rappeling line, but found none. A glance across the alley assured him the abandoned apartment building standing even with the warehouse was still empty.

The four terrorist vehicles ran close together. Bright splotches denoting James's pistol accuracy decorated their tops in glowing irregular spills to the NVGs.

Katz inhaled through his nose, blowing his inner tension out through his mouth. A calm descended over him as the terrorists entered the trap Phoenix had set.

The lead van was almost at the mouth of the alley, about to pull onto another street toward the Yad Vashem. In the rear the other van had just entered the alley.

Katz hit the transmit button. "Gary, you may announce our presence now."

A powerful engine revved, then a transmission groaned in protest. Without warning and without lights a dump truck screamed across the mouth of the alley, turned inward to connect with the nose of the van and smashed the terrorist vehicle against the back of the empty apartment building. The crash of rending metal echoed between the buildings and reached Katz's ears.

Manning hit the door, leaped into the street and took cover beside the warehouse before the terrorists could overcome their surprise and free themselves from the wreckage of their vehicle.

Men carrying assault rifles spilled from the twisted van. Some of them limped and held hands to their heads or arms. Two of them stumbled and fell to the ground. Yelled warnings punctuated the panicked autofire that chipped brick splinters from the buildings.

The second van slammed into the rear of the station wagon before it could stop. The Land Rover started to reverse in an attempt to clear the alley.

Katz tapped the transmit button. "Rafael."

In answer a bulldozer came around the corner of the alley with the scoop lowered like a battering ram. Sheets of tarp that had kept it covered were chewed from the bulldozer by the huge tracks. The scoop caught the rest of the Land

Rover and barreled into it. Metal buckled and glass imploded. Lifted free of the ground, the all-terrain vehicle seemed to fold up on itself like an accordion.

"Gary," Katz radioed.

"Go," Manning answered.

"Stage two."

"Coming right up. Fire in the hole!"

Katz looked at the apartment building opposite the warehouse. Thunder collected behind the walls, rolling in a destructive cadence. There was an impression of little lightning bolts, then the upper third of the building sheared away and came raining down in huge chunks across the trapped vehicles. Though pressed for time, the Canadian demolitions man had once again proved what an artist he was at his craft.

Terrorists went down under blocks of brick and mortar and didn't move again. More debris settled across the vehicles and broke their metallic backs.

"Gary," Katz called.

"In position."

"Rafael."

"In position."

"Calvin."

"I'm over the hump now."

Katz looked and saw the ex-SEAL come tumbling down a shelf of brick, the man's uniform marked with a large *X* across the front and back of his blacksuit that only the NVGs could pick up.

Bright flares of the terrorist weapons raked the night without finding true targets. The men, lost in chaos, fired at shadows.

Nodding to McCarter, Katz took his place on the building's eave, turned around, let the rope take his weight, then rappelled down using the one-handed braking system. McCarter's Uzi came to life beside him, unleashing burst after burst of 9 mm parabellums that left his targets down and dead. Katz hit the wall with his booted feet, kicked out again immediately and kept going.

Once he was on the ground, the Israeli raked the Ka-bar combat knife from his harness and slashed through the rappelling rig. McCarter took the right, Katz the left, his Uzi up and spitting controlled fire.

Closing in on the line of wrecked cars, Katz used figure-eight bursts on anything that moved. He cataloged faces automatically. Some he didn't know. The ones he did fitted in with the terrorist package from Stony Man.

Ijzim wasn't to be found. Yet.

The Phoenix Force leader stepped over a corpse as he shoved the Uzi under his right arm, dropped the empty clip and rammed home a fresh one. A shadow blurred into being before him, wreathed in the rising smoke from the broken cars. A bruising force expended itself against the Kevlar vest over his stomach. His breath froze in his lungs as the pain seized him. Then he watched the guy's head come apart as Encizo or Manning took the terrorist down from their sniping position.

"The lead car, Yakov," Encizo called quietly, "doesn't have Ijzim in it."

Katz whipped a withering burst through another man, then let the Uzi hang from its sling while he freed a grenade from his combat harness. Using an underhanded throw, he flipped the explosive through an empty window. He back-pedaled from the immediate vicinity, hitting the transmit button on his headset long enough to pass a warning on to McCarter, then took up the Uzi again.

For one frozen moment the scene inside the car looked like something from a tragicomedy. At least three men remained inside the van. All of them were groping for the grenade in the shadows filling the vehicle. Then an explosion mushroomed, too large for the van to hold. More corpses and ripped sections from the van joined the debris lining the alley.

The deafening thunderclap was penetrated by the keening wail of sirens signaling the approach of Israeli police or military forces.

Katz zipped a burst from sternum to forehead on a terrorist who had just recognized him as the enemy. He keyed the headset mike. "Thirty seconds inside the hellzone, then break off the engagement with or without Ijzim," he said tersely. "Gary, you have the count."

"Affirmative."

Breaking into a jog, Katz followed along in the destructive wake left by McCarter, administering cleanup shots on single-fire as needed. Not much was.

The station wagon was a chewed-up piece of metal already warped by the falling wall. Nothing moved inside. More dead littered the ground.

"Got him!" James said triumphantly.

Katz looked down the line of cars and saw James reach inside the crumpled Land Rover's door and drag a man out by his shirt collar. Another terrorist slithered through the passenger side window and took aim at the Phoenix warrior with a pistol.

Firing from the hip, Katz trailed a long burst that ripped through the shattered windshield and thin metal of the Rover's top. The terrorist jumped as the bullets struck home. The pistol shot was wide of the mark. Then the corpse dropped behind the Rover.

Ijzim looked worn and ragged, his clothing torn from the crash and from rough handling.

McCarter's Uzi blazed and two more terrorists went spinning away, clearing the field.

Katz was surprised to see James release his hostage, then saw the long shimmer of edged steel in Ijzim's hand. Bringing the Uzi up on single-shot, Katz aimed deliberately at the back of Ijzim's head, waiting to get a clear opportunity. Despite the wealth of information the terrorist chief possessed, the Phoenix Force leader wasn't about to lose one of his men for it. Keio Ohara had been enough.

Ijzim screamed and rushed James. Unable to get the shot he wanted, Katz had to watch and pray.

Moving with grace and speed, still holding his assault weapon in one hand, James stepped inside Ijzim's sweeping knife hand, pivoted and hit the terrorist with a backfist full of Uzi. Ijzim dropped in an unmoving heap before the sound of the meaty impact reached Katz's ears.

"You people are clear," Manning said, "and you're out of time. Now haul ass before we get busted for littering. Rafael and I have rear guard."

"How is he?" McCarter asked James as the three men zeroed in on Ijzim.

"Alive." James knelt and used a pair of plastic disposable cuffs to secure the terrorist's hands.

Katz kicked the knife away.

"Bloody bastard," McCarter said as he helped James raise Ijzim into a fireman's carry. "I'd have killed him if he'd pulled that friggin' knife on me."

James grinned. "Figured I'd rather take a chance with Ijzim than wait for Katz to skin me later for killing him."

Katz patted James on the shoulder and said, "You did well, Calvin," then took the lead, guiding them out of the twisted wreckage and debris. Much had been accomplished, but other cards still remained to be played before they could quit Jerusalem.

Behind them, coming closer, the sirens screamed into the night.

11

The noonday sun glared down mercilessly over Carl Lyons. He stood atop the luxury hotel and tried to make the meager shade offered by the huge HVAC systems stretch to contain him. There was no relief. It was one of those rare Miami days when the temperature hovered around ninety and the humidity was out of sight.

Away from the civilian world that drifted through the seventeen floors below him, he didn't have to worry about his weapons showing. The blond ex-cop was dressed in a light gray suit, and the .357 and .45 rode in shoulder leather that was as uncomfortable as it could get. He carried the summer-weight jacket in one hand while he peered out over the Miami Beach area.

Biscayne Bay rolled blue and slow behind the hotel, bisecting the eight-mile line of hotels, motels, villas, apartments and shops from its mirror image on the other bank. Palm trees and foliage were thicker on the west side of the bay. The dark green was welcome relief from the white buildings dotting the landscape. A few boats were berthed along the banks. The Dade County Sheriff's office and Coast Guard had joined forces early that morning to shut down the tourist action.

Using the binoculars that hung around his neck, Lyons could see the Collins Avenue causeway that was the primary link to the mainland. But he couldn't see the Miami PD undercover units assigned to check suspicious vehicles entering Miami Beach. Coast Guard ships patrolled the ocean waters east of the island. Lyons had counted at least five of them during the past two hours. Helicopter patrols hovered over the vicinity, radio-linked to the ground and water units maintaining the security perimeters.

Personally Lyons didn't figure any of the defensive measures would stand up to the test. Over the years he'd learned that anyone marked for assassination would be better off digging a hole somewhere no one knew them, then pulling the hole in after them. It was what had kept Salman Rushdie alive for so long.

The people downstairs were betting their lives that the increased public awareness of their impending doom would make them new favorites in the presidential polls. The only concession the political hopefuls had agreed to was in moving the announced televised debate to the fifteenth floor instead of holding it in one of the banquet rooms on the ground floor.

And that had only been after their lawyers had been convinced by the Dade County D.A.'s office that any innocent onlooker harmed by a terrorist attack could lodge complaints against the candidates for creating an unrestrained and dangerous atmosphere with their presence.

That bit of legal clout had been instigated by Barbara Price to the D.A.'s office via the Department of Justice. From what Price had said the D.A. and company hadn't been too gracious about complying. By enforcing the pressure on the politicians, they were ruffling feathers and endangering future political favor on the home ground.

With presidential candidates still turning up dead all across the country, Lyons figured everybody still standing at this point must look pretty good to somebody. There had even been announcements of new candidates throwing their hats into the ring.

The ear-throat headset squawked for attention as Lyons's mood threatened to become even more sour. The only good news that had reached him lately was the information concerning Leo Turrin's recovery in the hospital. The resilient little Fed was already being moved to a safehouse maintained by Stony Man operatives where he and his family would be taken care of.

Lyons hit the transmit button. "Go."

"Wizard," Schwarz said.

Booting the frequency up to the special one established for the Able Team members in the operation, Lyons said, "Here."

"Festivities are really starting to jump on the fourteenth, ironman. You might want to take a peek."

"Did you say 'take a puke'?"

"That, too." Schwarz cleared.

Lyons shrugged into his jacket and brushed the sweaty lapels back into place. A shadow drifted over him, momentarily eclipsing him from the sun. Startled, he looked up.

The dirigible hung like a fat silver cigar against the blue sky. Even in the distance Lyons could read the motor oil advertisement on its side. He'd noticed it earlier, too, and had thought briefly about the crew as they went about their efforts to break into the Guinness Book of World Records for the longest recorded dirigible flight. Of course, the owners were also selling their effort as one of the biggest and most attention-getting billboards in American history. Lyons had figured the guys on board were enjoying something like a long vacation. And he'd been a little envious, he had to admit.

Using the special magnetic passcard he'd been issued, he keyed the lock to the rooftop door, gave up on the elevator that had been commandeered by the law-enforcement people and subsequently been tied up to the tune of interdepartment disorder, and took the stairs. The stairwell access from the roof was covered by four hard cops he'd met earlier. They didn't check the badge and photo ID hanging from his jacket pocket. They didn't smile, either. He and the rest of Able Team enjoyed a freedom in the security net that the other agencies didn't understand or appreciate.

Schwarz met him in the landing at fourteen. "What's up?" Lyons asked.

"Blood pressure," Schwarz said. "Gonna boil the mercury if this keeps up."

The corridor on fourteen was filled with television, radio and journalism people all trying to talk at once. Lyons had met most of them earlier that morning while the security interviews were conducted. Electrical cables lay like fat, sleeping pythons across the plush carpet, and ran into the suite of rooms that had been combined by the hotel people for the political debate. Black electrical tape marred some of the cables in places. A few of the non-TV newspeople had taken knives to the cables when no one was looking. The sabotage had stopped when police officers were assigned to protect the cables, and after a magazine reporter accidently cut through a power line instead of a transmission line and ended up with a quick trip to the hospital.

Aside from the general chaos that Lyons had almost gotten used to, something else had been added. A line of people were filing into the south door of the suite. The looks on the faces of the cops working the orderly insertion of the group showed they were intensely displeased with the circumstances.

"Who are they?" Lyons asked.

"Citizens," Schwarz replied. A faint, mirthless grin touched his lips. "The 'god-fearing, apple-pie kind of American who won't mind kicking a little terrorist butt when the going gets tough.'"

Lyons glanced at his teammate. "Avery Jestro."

"The very guy," Schwarz agreed. "State congressman extraordinaire, staunch supporter of the flag, and Florida's favorite son to hear him tell it. And if you're around him, you get to hear it all the time."

"Yeah, I know." Lyons nodded toward the people. "So what's the story here? I thought it was agreed to keep civilians out of the line of fire."

"Because of the threat of lawsuits Jestro came up with a way of circumnavigating that."

"I'm all ears."

"He ran down to the lobby, borrowed a typewriter from the hotel staff and wrote up a form that said anyone who signed it—if wounded or killed during the debate—would forfeit all legal recourse because they were acting on their own recognizance."

"You're kidding."

"Nope." Schwarz crossed his heart. "Claimed he got the idea from redneck bars that have those mechanical bulls."

"Son of a bitch." Lyons watched the line of people continue to stream into the room.

"After he returned the typewriter, Jestro paid a clerk to run off duplicates on a copier. Then he had a couple of aides pass them out to the people in the street."

"Isn't there any way the hotel staff can keep them out?"

"Not yet. The only good thing is that the PD's called in the fire marshal and limited the number of people who can be in the suite at one time."

"How many civilians are we talking about?"

"Just over two hundred."

"Son of a bitch," Lyons said with more feeling.

"It's standing room only in there now, guy."

"Jestro needs to have his ass kicked up between his shoulder blades."

"You'd lose a lot of points in the popular opinion polls, Ironman. Right now Avery Jestro is a goddamn hero to the masses. Ranks right up there with Santa Claus."

"The bastard's rank all right," Lyons agreed. He moved through the corridor, paused to let a motel attendant push a cart of metal folding chairs into the suite, then followed the guy in.

The actual floor space available to the debating presidential hopefuls was severely limited by the crowd, security people and media. They sat in a line at the far end of the room, facing the gathering crowd. Windows overlooking the eastern shore of Miami Beach and the ocean lined the east wall. A helicopter darted past as Lyons watched. The floor space and area over the candidates scheduled to speak were filled with recording equipment. A wall of cameras faced them.

From the setup Lyons saw the media people had been given the front rows. Hotel attendants continued to assemble more rows for the public. It was filling up quick.

Lyons glanced back at the politicians. Jestro sat near the middle of them, looking overweight and pompous as he waved to his new admirers.

"Scratch the kick," Lyons said to Schwarz. "We need to bring back tar and feathers." He shrugged his shoulders in a vain attempt to loosen the tightness between them. "How long before this dog-and-pony show starts?"

"Ten minutes."

Lyons figured it would be a race to see whether the hotel attendants were able to seat the crowd before silence was demanded by the media. The attendants beat the time clock by a shade over forty seconds.

Leaning back against the wall, Lyons watched as the show opened dramatically, the announcer describing at length how all of the politicians at the debate had shown up de-

pite threats against their lives. Then there was a break for
tation identification and a couple of commercials.

The air-conditioning couldn't meet the demand. Lyons
abandoned his tie and opened his shirt collar, thinking it was
all the hot air in the room that killed the comfort zone.
Schwarz stayed beside him, alert to the various comings and
goings of the people inside the room. Blancanales stood two
doors down, looking fit in his suit and not at all bothered by
the rising heat.

On their special frequency Blancanales transmitted, "I
was downstairs when they started letting people in. There
was no way the police officers could check everyone who
entered the hotel."

"So you're telling me we have a lot of ciphers in here with
us?" Lyons said.

"Yeah."

"While you were down there," Schwarz asked, "did you
happen to see anyone looking suspicious?"

Across the room an honest smile lit Pol's face. "With the
situation being what it is, Gadgets, there wasn't *anyone* who
didn't look suspicious. Hell, you would have looked suspicious to me about then."

Lyons checked out of his teammates' conversation and
homed in on the beautiful television reporter asking Jestro
about his candidacy funding. Her name was Dianne Caitland, one of the locals. Apparently she'd discovered something wasn't exactly kosher about the congressman's dona-
tions from concerned supporters.

Lyons loved watching Jestro squirm around for an answer, clearing his throat repeatedly.

Brusque and efficient, Caitland didn't pause to give the
man time to think on his feet. She pursued her answer with
the intensity of a piranha scenting blood.

In the end Jestro was saved by the first explosion that
rocked the motel. Window glass shattered, some of it fall-

ing into the room and creating a fluid panic that raced through the crowd. As a flesh-and-blood mass, the three-hundred-plus people in the suite of rooms pushed away from the broken and empty windows and rushed for the four exits.

Lyons had the Colt Python in his fist but found himself pressed up against the wall by the stampeding people. Unwilling to hurt anyone, unable to find any sign of an enemy, he struggled just enough to keep himself on his feet. Blancanales and Schwarz were lost from sight. The uniforms of the Miami PD were washed out of the room with the human tide.

Cameramen went down, still running film. Microphones were torn and flung from their temporary moorings. Metal folding chairs were overturned, then people tripped over them in the frenzied rush for safety.

Lyons switched the headset to the Able Team channel and keyed the transmit button. "Where the hell did that come from?"

Before Schwarz or Blancanales could reply another explosion shuddered through the hotel. This time Lyons could sense the direction. It came from the floors above, but it didn't feel like a planted explosive. If it had come from inside the structure, the concussion would have been directed more downward. This had felt as if it had come from outside the building.

"Ironman," Schwarz called.

"Go." Lyons pushed away from the wall, helped an old woman with a bloody nose to her feet, then passed her off to a sheriff's deputy heading to the hallway to work crowd control.

"Change freqs to the Coast Guard channel," Gadgets said. "They've spotted a fishing boat out there shelling the hotel."

Lyons made the adjustment as he forced his way through the crowd. Static and other communications stepped on one another and cluttered the channel. In the open now, he made his way through the maze of scattered chairs and broken glass. Blood on the carpeted floor testified that some people had been injured.

A third explosion slammed into the hotel, rocking it again. More glass dropped from the broken windows.

Taking his binoculars from his jacket pocket, Lyons scanned the ocean. He identified the suspect fishing boat from the three Coast Guard cutters zeroing in on it.

"Got some kind of three-inch or five-inch gun on board," a Coast Guard captain said before the interference covered the transmission again.

A puff of smoke appeared on the bow of the fishing boat. A few heartbeats later another round impacted against the side of the hotel. Concrete, steel and glass peeled away from the building and started the long fall to the street.

Lyons rode out the shock wave, listening to the frantic radio communications from the Coast Guard ships. He could hear their deck guns yammering in the background, interrupted by the demands of land-based law-enforcement chiefs demanding to know what the hell was going on and why the Coast Guard hadn't neutralized the problem by now.

A diving shape came from the sky's upper deck. Lyons figured the pilot was working a separate frequency because he never heard the guy coming. The terrorists aboard the fishing boat never turned their gun from the hotel. The fifth round thundered into the top of the building.

Then a sudden eruption of missile fire spread across the ocean's surface. One moment the fishing boat was there; in the next only burning and charred wood floated in the oil slick where the boat had vanished.

The Navy F-14 Tomcat twirled low over the water as the pilot pulled out of the steep dive. The fighter plane shot by low over Miami Beach and left the hammering of taxed jet engines echoing over Biscayne Bay.

Lyons dumped the Coast Guard channel and jumped back to the Able Team frequency as he went into motion. "Pol. Gadgets." The room was empty now, but he could still see civilians and law-enforcement people milling around out in the hallway. Someone had pulled the fire alarm, and its warning mixed in with the screams and shouts of the panicked crowd.

"Here," Blancanales answered.

"Here," Schwarz said.

"The sea-based assault's been erased," Lyons said as he bulled his way through to the stairwell.

"Good to know," Blancanales said, "but we're still looking at a hell of a lot of damage and injury with this mob evacuation."

"And it's not exactly to our benefit to have so many guys running around with guns right now," Schwarz added. "These people see a rifle or pistol, they figure you for a bad guy and it complicates matters even more."

Lyons made the stairwell, fought across the crush of people funnelling down the flights of stairs and found himself quickly crushed against the wall. Having the Python visible barely bought him breathing room. He hit the transmit button and had to talk loud to be heard. "Anybody besides me think that those guys on that boat must have had incredibly bad targeting abilities to miss the fourteenth floor five times in a row?"

"I've been thinking about that," Blancanales said, "but I didn't come up with any answers. They banged the hell out of the top of the building, though."

"Yeah," Lyons said. "Maybe it's that old suspicious cop's mind of mine at work, but I have to ask myself why."

"I wasn't a cop," Schwarz said, "but I've been in plenty of firefights. It scans wrong to me, too. If this isn't a suck of some kind, Ironman, I'll eat your hat."

The unmistakable sound of gunshots came from below. It started as widely spaced hollow pops, then turned into roaring autofire.

Lyons stripped out of his jacket, allowing freer access to his combat rig. He tapped the transmit button. "Gadgets, Pol, anything?"

"Negative," Schwarz said.

"It's coming from your end of the building," Blancanales said.

Holstering the Python, Lyons forced his way to the stairs among the frozen crowd reacting to the unexpected menace obviously waiting below. He threw a leg over the railing and started climbing down the inside of the stairwell. His tennis shoes slipped occasionally, but he went as quickly as he could, stretching his body to the limit to cover the distance efficiently.

"Officer!" a man on the ninth-floor landing called out. A dead man, his hands partially covering his bloody face, lay halfway in the doorway leading to the ninth-floor corridor. None of the crowd seemed willing to step over the corpse despite the way the people in the back kept shoving.

Lyons clambered back onto the landing and swept the Python from leather. "What happened?" he asked the man. Now that he was closer he could see the blood spatters that had hit the man's white shirt.

"A group of men," the man said. "Terrorists. They had to be. They were waiting here. Other people went on down. Those men, they grabbed Dianne Caitland, the reporter. They grabbed her and two or three others. This man, he tried to stop them. They shot him."

Gripping the .357 Magnum in both hands, Lyons swung around the doorway and covered the corridor with the muzzle. A group of stunned people tried to find cover against the walls or went to ground. None of them had weapons.

"They went that way," a teenage boy said.

Lyons broke into a run, tracked the new thunder of autofire ripping through the hallway and yelled at the civilians to clear the area. He paused for just a moment at the doors reserved for the room service employees. Planting a big foot on the door, he followed it through.

A muzzle-flash flared out from the darkness. Garish red lights from the soft drink machine colored the terrorists' faces.

Lyons targeted the first man, the Python bucking in his fists. There was an impression of a darker red spreading over the man's face, then the impact of the bullet jerked the terrorist's head backward.

Two rounds from the second terrorist slammed into Lyons's bulletproof vest. Going with the impacts, the Able Team fighter sprawled backward onto the floor. He rolled, caught himself on one hand and raised his pistol. Dropping the hammer three times, he blew the remaining terrorist against the wall and bounced him off it. The man rebounded to the floor after the last bullet struck him and stayed there.

As Lyons's nostrils filled with the scent of cordite trapped in the room, he hit the transmit button. "They had people inside the building," he said. "They're picking off preselected hostages from the crowds flooding the stairwells and elevators. They're ahead of us on the way back to street level."

"Understood, Ironman," Blancanales responded, "but there's not a hell of a lot I can do from here. I'm boxed in by the people we're supposed to be protecting."

"Me, too," Schwarz added.

Lyons entered the hotel-staff stairwell cautiously, stepped ver the corpse of the sheriff's deputy who had been as- gned to it. He changed frequencies on the headset and tried raise the law-enforcement people. He only wasted his me. The channel was filled with chaos and misinforma- on.

He clicked out without reaching anyone, then booted ack into the Able channel. Charging down the stairs with e .357 once more fully loaded, he went as quickly as pos- ible, acutely aware that the law-enforcement teams had een drawn into the suck and there wasn't a damn thing they ould do to pick up the pieces of the busted play.

AKOV KATZENELENBOGEN approached the Mossad car ith his hands well away from his body. He went armed. Despite the loose agreement he'd arranged, he was no fool.

The vehicle squatted in the shadows of the side street near affa Road. A moment before the Phoenix Force leader eached the car, the back door opened.

"Come inside, Yakov."

"I've got you on thermal imaging, Katz," Calvin James vhispered through the headset. "Just don't get so close to he guy that your patterns blur in the scope."

"Yes," Yakov said to both men. His teammates were here only to prevent any attempts at abduction. Their fight till wasn't with the Israelis. He slipped into the car and losed the door after him.

Elrad Morganstein sat on the other side of the back seat. A young driver with visible shoulder leather and a pump hotgun nosing over the seats watched Katz through the earview mirror.

"Once there was a time when my word would have been ood enough to convince you I meant you no harm, El- ad," Katz said.

Morganstein glanced at him with tired brown eyes. "That time is passed, Yakov, as is the time when I could be certain of your loyalty to my country."

The words hurt Katz, but he kept his pain from his face. "I have Ijzim and Maimun."

"So the work near the Yad Vashem was that of you and your people."

"Yes."

"The terrorist bastards were on their way to destroy the monument?"

Katz nodded.

Sighing, Morganstein turned his gaze back toward the front of the car. "You took chances that weren't yours to take."

"I took chances to protect a land that I love very much, old friend."

"I wish I could believe you."

"That's between you and your heart, Elrad. Perhaps the threat of war has hardened it so much that you can no longer see the truth."

"I'm beginning to think the truth extends no farther than Israel's borders."

Katz fell silent. As in the old days when Morganstein was confronted by answers that pulled him in two opposing directions, the man had to take his own time to choose which course to follow.

"You say you have Maimun and Ijzim?"

"Yes."

"Alive?"

"Yes."

"And what do you want for them?"

"Nothing."

Disbelief shone in Morganstein's eyes. "Won't you even ransom them for free passage through Jerusalem?"

"No. My team and I have our own way."

The driver turned around forcefully. "You haven't made it out of this car yet, old man."

Katz met the driver's gaze without comment.

Morganstein raised his voice and spoke harshly. "If you interrupt this conversation again, Ira, I'll see you brought up on charges. Is that clear?"

The driver nodded, but hot fires gleamed in his eyes.

"It's good that you don't seek to bargain for your freedom," Morganstein said. "I'm not empowered to guarantee anything like that."

"I understand." Katz pulled the key from around his neck and broke the string that held it. He dangled it out for Morganstein to take, then dropped it into the man's palm. "You'll find them locked in the dumpster in that alley." He pointed. "They've been sedated but should come around in an hour or so. You'll also find a pack of documents and maps with them, giving intelligence about the known terrorist cell operating within the city. Since Maimun, Ijzim and Nejd have been eliminated, your people should have an easier time picking them off. By morning the interior threat to Israel should be nullified."

"Thanks to you and your unnamed group."

Katz didn't respond to the obvious sarcasm. He slipped out of the car, stood by the open door and felt uncertain. "It was better this way, Elrad."

"We could have cleaned our own house, Yakov. We've been looking out for ourselves for a very long time."

"It was felt that the paranoia sweeping through Israel would have been counterproductive to the elimination of the terrorist squads. Perhaps if we'd had all the information we now possess earlier, things could have been worked out differently."

Morganstein pocketed the key. "It's too late for maybes."

Katz nodded and closed the door, feeling the ache of the loss rattle inside him.

"Yakov."

He turned and saw the car's rear window rolled down and Morganstein leaning out of it. He waited while the man joined him, then followed him well away from the car.

"Perhaps," Morganstein said with the light from a streetlamp making his features stark and bloodless, "your own house isn't so clean, either."

"I don't know what you're talking about."

Morganstein hesitated, then reached a decision. "Over an hour ago a commando attack was launched against a secret nuclear installation near Tel Aviv. Two nuclear bombs were taken away before the military could cordon off the area. It was obvious that the raiders were intimate with the installation and what was kept there."

"The Iraqis couldn't have done something like that," Katz said. "If they'd penetrated the perimeters of the installation and gotten to the bombs, they'd have set them off."

"There were two bodies recovered at the site."

Katz waited, possibilities already churning through his mind, trying to figure out why the Russians would take the chance.

"Both men appear to be Americans."

"It can't be."

"But it is," Morganstein said. "We should know who they were by morning."

"It makes no sense."

"Yet it has happened. It appears no one has true allies in this war." Morganstein hugged Katz to him fiercely, then released him and walked away. "Goodbye, old friend. I shall miss you."

Katz stepped into the shadows as confusion flooded him. Questions and impossible answers cycled through his mind. Whoever had masterminded the raid had succeeded in snatching a large defeat from the jaws of a small victory.

within Israel. If it was true that an American force had been behind the mission, there was nothing that could hold back aggressive Israeli involvement in the war with Iraq. A true world war could sweep over the globe within hours.

12

Watching the computer screens on Aaron Kurtzman's desk flicker and juice information, Barbara Price tried to sort out everything Hal Brognola was telling her about Operation Toyworx.

Katz's communication had come into Stony Man Farm only moments ago.

"So we probably *are* behind the nuclear arms snatch," Price said into the headset's curving mike.

"Maybe," Brognola acknowledged, "but not directly. It looks as if someone might have been using the information compiled through Toyworx. From what Aaron's been able to pick up from the Israeli security net, it definitely resembles a scenario worked out by the Pentagon during last year's war."

A picture of a young man with a military crew cut came up on one of the computer screens. The sheen over his eyes held only death. A window opened beside it, revealing another man who looked American and military. Kurtzman's fingers played over the keyboard, piling programming commands for cybernetic search and seizure into the system.

"We've got pictures of the dead men," Price said. "Aaron's running them now."

"That's more than they've got here in Wonderland," Brognola told her. "You need to work the intel and the pictures into the American espionage net as soon as you can leave Stony Man out of it.''

''Uh-uh,'' Price said. ''I want to sit on these for a while. Once the Pentagon gets hold of it, the intel will be spread out for everyone to access. I want a few hours' lead time to put the finger on the people responsible for this.''

''Agreed. I'm sure the Man will go along. He wants this quashed as soon as we can. The question of American involvement regarding Israeli security and nuclear weapons is going to jeopardize the working relationship we have with our allies.''

Price watched the computer search kick into play, scanning through thousands of documents in seconds.

''What about Phoenix?'' Brognola asked.

''They're pulling out of Israel as planned,'' Price replied. ''The mission there is finished. The Mossad has Ijzim and Maimun, as well as the intel we had on the rest of the terrorist cell. They should be able to take them out without stressing the relations with the Palestinians any further.''

''Where are they going?''

''Kuwait. They're linking up with Striker to consolidate the Desert Lightning position. The more behind-the-lines strikes we can muster, the more effective the allies' counterstrike will be when it comes.'' She glanced at her watch. The allied bombing raid was scheduled seventeen minutes from now. She wondered if Striker had made the meet, wondered if he'd be safe when death started dropping from the sky.

The phone line buzzed. She glanced at the lighted board and saw that it was the private line for Able Team. Putting Brognola on hold, she switched over.

''Barb,'' Lyons said tiredly, ''things have gone all to hell down here.''

Price had already seen news footage covering the shelling of the hotel. She hadn't known about the hostages. Taking a manila folder from one side of the desk, she flipped it open and stared at the stark images of the homeless people who'd been sheathed in flames only hours ago.

"It's time to come home, Ironman," she said. "While you people have been down there, Aaron cracked more of the computer files we recovered from the New York angle. The attack on the homeless within the D.C. area was part of a scheme designed to split up the law-enforcement departments in the city. With public pressure on the President's going to be giving a news conference tomorrow. He's their real target, and they might have someone on the inside. Let the Miami PD take care of following up the leads down there until we have something solid to hang on to."

Lyons was silent for a moment. "This is a tough one to give up, lady."

"You're *not* giving it up," Price said with conviction. "You're just putting it on a back burner till you have something to go on." She paused for emphasis. "You people are needed here, Carl. I have a jet waiting on you."

"You're right," Lyons said. "Keep a light on for us."

"It's already there." Price broke the connection and returned to Brognola. "You've been following the action in Miami?"

"Yeah. Apparently the Coast Guard took out the terrorists."

Price updated him on what had actually happened.

"How many hostages?" Brognola asked.

"They're not sure. It's all still being sorted out down there. Some have been confirmed, but it's going to be hard to say for a few hours yet. Pandemonium's still filling the streets around the hotel."

"Able Team?"

"Whole," Price replied, "and on their way back."

"Anything from Striker?"

"Not yet. We've checked the channel through Grimaldi. It's still operative. At this point we're waiting on him."

"Barb."

Price glanced at Kurtzman and saw the big man staring at the computer screen before him with a look of intense distaste. CONFIRMATION blinked across the top and bottom of the screen.

"We've just ID'ed the two men shot down in Tel Aviv," Kurtzman said. "And they're us."

Price looked and read the scrolled message identifying the men as part of Toyworx and as a part of the Desert Lightning unit. "Shit. There's got to be some kind of mistake." She looked at Kurtzman.

The big man shook his head. "No mistake. We've found the enemy, and they're us."

She relayed the news to Brognola, trying to figure out what the hell it meant. "Break into the Desert Lightning com/net," she told Kurtzman. "Get me a link with Eldridge. We've got to get to the bottom of this now, before the Israelis get wind of it."

Kurtzman's hands flew across the keyboard.

Switching Brognola to the speaker box, Price picked up the headset and listened to the connection being made through the commando unit's special frequency.

"Desert Lightning Base, this is Whistler. Over." The code name was for emergency use only. The Desert Lightning radio personnel knew it was an eyes-only communique.

"Roger, Whistler, you have Desert Lightning Base. Over."

"Base, Whistler needs to speak with Desert Lightning Two. Over."

"Sorry, Whistler, Base can't comply. Two isn't here. Over."

"Give me the most senior officer you have within reach, Base. Over."

"Whistler," a new voice said less than a minute later, "this is Desert Lightning Four. Can I help you? Over."

Calming herself with effort, Price thumbed the transmit button. "Affirmative, Four. You can comply by telling me the status of Two. Over."

"Two's gone," the man said in a perplexed tone. "According to orders that were faxed to him under your code name, Two split the unit in half, then took his group with him to approach Iraq. Is there a problem? Over."

"No problem, Four. Whistler out."

Kurtzman killed the connection and stared at her.

Price dropped the headset on the desk and leaned heavily onto it, staring at the map of the Middle East on the wall screen at the far end of the room and wondering how the hell things had gone so wrong. The thing that scared her most was that she was seasoned enough to know not to believe the busted plays would end there.

CLAD IN A BLACK NIGHTSUIT and using the shadows as part of his defense, Mack Bolan closed in on the meet site ten minutes ahead of schedule. Talia Alireza was somewhere behind him.

He wore a Kevlar vest. As usual, the Desert Eagle rode on his right hip, and the Beretta 93-R was snugged in shoulder leather. An arsenal clung to his combat harness, and he carried the MAC-10 in his right hand.

As he walked, he dipped his free hand into the canvas pouch at his waist. Each time he came up with a radio-controlled explosive coupled with a smoke charge, then tossed it to one side or the other of the winding alley. It was his escape route if things went badly, and he had every turn marked in his mind. When the pouch was empty, he tossed it behind an abandoned garbage can.

He waited in the mouth of the alley, peering out over the empty street where Semyon Zagladin was to meet him. The numbers trickled through the warrior's mind. The KGB agent had chosen the site well.

This part of Baghdad still showed signs of last year's allied bombing efforts. Buildings stood humbled and broken, chunks of mortar and brick dragged to the sides of the street in an effort to clear one lane. There hadn't been much time for domestic housekeeping with Khalid Shawiyya replacing Saddam Hussein as Iraq's president. And then the efforts had bent more toward preparing for the next outbreak of violence than in recovering from the first.

The city held lifetimes of old scars, Bolan knew. More were going to be added tonight, and there wasn't anything that could stop that. The warrior felt bad about not telling Talia Alireza what was coming, but it couldn't be helped. The struggle within her was hard enough. He wished there was some way he could help her, then wondered at his own thoughts. It was pretty egotistical on his part. Views, if truly believed in, had to be reached from within an individual, not given to them.

His combat senses quivered to alertness seconds before he heard the whisper of tire rubber on concrete. Shifting in the shadows, he tapped the headset. "Valkyrie."

"I'm with you."

"It's show time."

"I see them."

A long black American limousine pulled through the intersection, dimmed its lights and came to a stop across the street.

"Anyone with them?" Bolan asked.

"I don't see anyone," the woman responded, "but that doesn't mean they aren't there."

"Understood." Bolan waited, glanced at his watch and saw that the bombing run was scheduled to start less than five minutes away. Zagladin was late.

A man jumped out on the passenger side, carrying an AK-47 canted over his shoulder. His movement was crisp, military. He opened the back door.

Semyon Zagladin stepped out of the car wearing a trench coat that didn't fit in with the night's warmth. Bolan immediately assumed the KGB agent was wearing bulletproof armor under the coat.

"There are four men still inside the vehicle," Alireza whispered into his ear. "From the way it's riding low on the tires, I'm betting the limo is armored and has been equipped with bulletproof glass."

"Affirmative."

Zagladin spread his hands and smiled. He was a big man, an even bigger target. The arm waving was supposed to be a subliminal invitation to shoot at his chest. The trouble was, the Executioner had already seen through the subterfuge.

"I thought we were here for a meeting," Zagladin called from across the street.

Bolan keyed the transmit button. "No matter what happens," he said quietly, "if anything breaks out, Zagladin goes down first."

"Yes." Alireza sounded cool, calm.

The Executioner stepped out into the street, letting the moonlight hit him. Less than thirty feet separated him from Zagladin. "Not a meeting," he said. "I've come to deliver a message." He was aware of the second hand on his watch counting down the minutes.

"How very American," Zagladin said with heavy sarcasm. "John Wayne would be proud. However, I was told we'd talk, perhaps reach some agreement regarding our joint interests in the Middle East."

"A Soviet presence won't be accepted here now or later," Bolan told him.

"You people have gotten increasingly greedy under your latest president," Zagladin said in a cold voice. "You've interfered in a number of countries that didn't want the United States involved in their affairs. The Soviet Union isn't prepared to pull out of this place just because of a few threats."

"No threats," Bolan said in a graveyard tone. "That's a promise you can take to the bank. Whatever it takes, whatever it costs, the United States government isn't going to allow a Russian beachhead to become established here."

Zagladin started to speak.

Bolan went on before the other man could begin. "You and your people have been behind the deaths of Americans and their allies as much as Jaluwi and the terrorist organizations."

If Zagladin was surprised to learn that the secret about Jaluwi was out, he didn't show it.

"Soviet espionage circles owe a blood price for those lives, and it's going to be exacted," Bolan said. "The only option you people have is to back out."

"That's impossible," Zagladin replied.

Alireza whispered into Bolan's ear. "There's movement at ten o'clock."

Using his peripheral vision, the Executioner spotted the sniper moving atop the two-story building diagonal from him across the intersection.

"You Americans are a nation of dreamers," Zagladin said. "Your military bases in Kuwait are all but destroyed. The same has happened to the bases in Saudi Arabia. Terrorist death squads ride roughshod over your homeland. Israel, long your great friend and comrade in the Middle East, is on the verge of forsaking you. And you come here, full of piss and vinegar as you Americans say, and dare to take such a bold stance with Soviet forces."

"There are others," Alireza told Bolan in a tighter voice. "They're moving all around you, closing in on your position. You don't have time to waste. Get out of there."

"Does your president truly want to go to war here in the Middle East against such insurmountable odds?" Zagladin demanded.

"It's not so much a matter of wanting to," Bolan said. "It's more a matter of having to. With every step your espionage agencies and Jaluwi have taken to force the United States out of here, the harder you've made it for the American government to consider any alternative other than war."

Zagladin smiled. "Since we appear to be at an impasse, it occurs to me that one of my favorite American expressions would fit here. It looks as if it's time for your president to either fish or cut bait."

Without warning, the hollow booms of Iraqi mortar fire rumbled through the night. The sound spread over Baghdad, rolling in shock waves across the alley.

The Executioner was in motion at once. He dropped and rolled back into the shadows. A rifle bullet scored the brick wall behind where he'd been standing. The estimated trajectory indicated the sniper he'd spotted.

As he came to his feet, he drew the Desert Eagle and lifted it into target acquisition. Zagladin took a moment to draw his side arm, then tried to slip back into the limo.

"The President's quite a fisherman," Bolan shouted across the thirty-foot distance. "Figured you people would know that by now." The .44 Magnum boomed and bucked in his fist.

The 240-grain bullet plowed into the soft flesh and skull behind Zagladin's right ear, taking away most of the face on its way through. The corpse stumbled and fell over the open door. Blood spilled down the window.

Shifting targets, the Executioner was taking up the slack on the trigger when the man beside the limo flipped backward. Alireza had been slow in responding after the mortar fire opened up, but she was on target.

Antiaircraft fire rent the night, throwing a light show against the black sky. Orange and green tracer rounds from machine gun emplacements streaked through the sky.

Then the allied bombs started to fall, the ground quaking under their impacts. A mile away the skyline around the presidential palace began to take on a new configuration as buildings crumbled to the ground.

Leathering the Desert Eagle, Bolan turned and sprinted toward his escape route. A man using a corner of the alley for cover came into view, and the snout of an automatic rifle spit fire. The Executioner squeezed the MAC-10's trigger as he charged the man's position. The .45-caliber bullets raked the man from the wall, caught him again and punched him to the ground.

Bolan let instinct and memory guide him, reserving his conscious mind to zero in on the enemies surrounding him. He slapped the remote control on his combat harness. Immediately the charges he'd planted in the alley went off with percussions that sounded like hollow pops against the background of explosive carnage sweeping through Baghdad. Smoke spewed into the air, filling the alley in seconds.

"Goddamn you, Striker!" Alireza's voice shrieked into his ear. "You should have told me about this! I had a right to know!"

Ignoring her, Bolan ran on.

Only one other man confronted him in the alley. He didn't see the guy until he was almost on top of him. Zipping a quick burst that stitched the Russian from crotch to throat, he couldn't avoid slamming into the corpse, then went down in a tangle of arms and legs.

The sound of bombing went on, crashing and thundering across the city. Raging fires and tracers flying in all directions lit up Baghdad.

Pushing himself to his feet, he pumped his legs, driving his booted feet hard against the pavement. He changed clips

in the Ingram and swung out onto the first open street behind the alley. Footsteps pounded after him, trapped in their
own little world in his senses as the destruction covering the
city went on. The buildings in front of him seemed to shudder from the detonations of the bomb.

He freed a grenade from his harness and flipped it back
into the alley where it went off. Even if it hadn't caught any
of his pursuers, it would give them something to think
about.

As he crossed the street, the limo came around the corner, tires squealing with the effort of keeping traction.
Caught in the glare of the headlights, Bolan raised the
MAC-10, remembered the bulletproof glass and lowered the
muzzle. Squeezing the trigger, he aimed for the tires. One of
the headlights winked out and sparks jumped from the
street.

Undaunted, the big car rushed on like a metal shark cutting through calm water. A gunner leaned out a window.
Using the last few rounds in the clip, Bolan sliced across the
Russian agent's body with a trail of bullets that plucked the
guy from the car.

Waiting until the last possible moment, the Executioner
broke to his left, arching for the building that was the rendezvous point for Talia Alireza and him. His boot heel
slammed against the fender and numbed his leg. Off balance, he went spinning to the pavement, skin scraping from
his palms and one elbow. Before the pain could set in he
jerked a hand grenade from his harness, pulled the pin, held
the orb for a count of one and lobbed it underhanded toward the limo as it came around for another pass.

The grenade went off under the luxury car's engine, lifted
the front wheels clear of the street, then thumped them back
down again. White smoke billowed from under the hood.
Spiderweb cracks covered the windshield. The driver ground
the starter for a moment, then flames wavered into life from
the fender walls.

Two men made it clear of the limo before it blew. The top
of the car came free of the body and spiraled away like a
mammoth, flaming Frisbee.

Tracking one of the men, Bolan squeezed the trigger on
the newly charged MAC-10 and put his target down. As he
turned to face the surviving Russian, a triburst hammered
into his Kevlar vest and knocked him from his feet again.

He scrambled, heard the frantic autofire of the Russian
as the agent tried to confirm the kill, then heard a single shot
echo across the street. When he looked, the last Russian was
down and Alireza stood with her sniper rifle snugged into
her shoulder on the curb. Pushing himself to his feet, he
sprinted to her side, took her elbow and pulled her in the
direction of the planned escape route.

Allied bombs continued to pound the city.

"You should have told me," she said when they made
another corner. She stopped and jerked her arm from his
grasp. Anger and pain shone in her eyes. "You knew they
were planning to bomb the city. You knew it all along, didn't
you, you bastard?"

"Yes."

"You should have told me."

"I couldn't." Bolan glanced around the corner, making
sure they weren't being followed. The flames around the
limo climbed steadily, and it exploded again, but the sound
was lost in the drumming cadence produced by the aerial
bombing.

"There are innocents out there dying tonight," the
woman said. Her hands knotted around her rifle. "People
who are just as guiltless as the Americans gunned down in
the streets of their cities. Those allied soldiers are showing
as much compassion to those Iraqi innocents as the terrorists are in the United States."

"There's a difference," Bolan argued. "The man flying
those planes aren't stalking the innocent, trying to make
victims of them to back this country down. They're waging

war the only way they know how—to protect something they believe in.''

"And all these beliefs do is get people killed." Tears sparkled in her eyes. "That's what wars boil down to. Beliefs. Not right and wrong the way you Americans so proudly choose to view it."

"We don't have time for this," Bolan growled. "We've got to go."

"You go." She took the headset off, threw it to the ground, then turned and walked away from him. "I want nothing more of you or your war."

Silently Bolan watched her go, knowing in his warrior's heart that Talia Alireza hadn't truly made peace within herself before confronting the harsh realities of this coming war.

More allied thunder ripped into the city and made the ground shudder.

Having no choice, already on a tight schedule and unwilling to risk Grimaldi's hiding place any more than necessary, Bolan turned to go, heading in the other direction. If he made the rendezvous in time, he and Grimaldi would have an armed escort out of the country.

He listened for the sound of approaching footsteps as he went, hoping Talia Alireza would change her mind and join him.

But she didn't.

* * * * *

Don't miss the exciting conclusion of the Storm Trilogy. Look for SuperBolan #27, Storm Burst, in June.

**Welcome to Deathlands,
where you don't have to
die to go to hell.**

JAMES AXLER
DEATH LANDS ®
Chill Factor

Trekking through the ruins of a nuclear-devastated America, Ryan
Cawdor and his nomadic band of warrior-survivalists search for
the secrets of the past that might promise a future.

To rescue his young son enslaved in the frigid North, Ryan must
first face one of his oldest enemies—and play out the deadly fi-
nale to their private war.

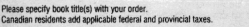